Praise for António Lobo Antunes

"His descriptive quickness and his genius for metaphor cause the line between prose and poetry to vanish before our astonished eyes." —Billy Collins, former U.S. poet laureate

"The greatest living Portuguese writer. . . . He has been compared to Céline . . . [but] he owes as much to Proust in the complexity of his style. One could also invoke Malcolm Lowry or Cormac McCarthy for the visionary power, the buried violence." —*Vogue* (Paris)

"One of the most skillful psychological portraitists writing anywhere." —*The New Yorker*

"Lobo Antunes is a writer completely at ease with every aspect of his enormous talent." —*The Observer* (London)

"A master navigator of the human psyche." —Jonathan Levi, *Los Angeles Times Book Review*

"A real original. No one else writes quite like him. . . . Extraordinarily vivid prose, the pages [are] alive with surreal images." —*Times Literary Supplement* (London)

The Land at the End of the World

Knowledge of Hell (1980)

An Explanation of the Birds (1981)

Fado Alexandrino (1983)

Acts of the Damned (1985)

The Return of the Caravels (1988)

The Natural Order of Things (1992)

The Inquisitors' Manual (1996)

What Can I Do When Everything's On Fire? (2008)

The Fat Man and Infinity (2009)

The Land at the End of the World

A NOVEL

António Lobo Antunes

TRANSLATED WITH AN INTRODUCTION BY

MARGARET JULL COSTA

 W. W. NORTON & COMPANY | NEW YORK | LONDON

Manufacturing by Courier Westford
Book design by JAM Design
Production manager: Devon Zahn

Library of Congress Cataloging-in-Publication Data

Antunes, António Lobo, 1942–
[Cus de Judas. English]
The land at the end of the world : a novel / António Lobo Antunes ;
translated with an introduction by Margaret Jull Costa.
    p. cm.
ISBN 978-0-393-07776-6
1. Angola—History—Revolution, 1961–1975—Fiction.
I. Costa, Margaret Jull. II. Title.
PQ9263.N77C813 2011
869.3'42—dc22

                                      2010051085

W. W. Norton & Company, Inc.
500 Fifth Avenue, New York, N.Y. 10110
www.wwnorton.com

W. W. Norton & Company Ltd.
Castle House, 75/76 Wells Street, London W1T 3QT

1 2 3 4 5 6 7 8 9 0

FOR MY FRIEND DANIEL SAMPAIO

Introduction

by Margaret Jull Costa

*A*ntónio Lobo Antunes is generally considered to be Portugal's greatest living writer and one of the most original voices in contemporary fiction. His biography is well known, but not necessarily to English-speaking readers. Born in 1942 in Benfica, then a suburb of Lisbon, Lobo Antunes was the oldest of six brothers. His sole ambition, from the age of seven, was to be a writer, but he was diverted from this path by his father, a professor of neurology, who advised him to study medicine instead—hoping, perhaps, to save his eldest son from what he imagined would be an impecunious future. The young António took his father's advice and chose psychiatry, which was, it seemed to him, the branch of medicine most closely allied to literature. After qualifying in 1968, he worked as an intern in a London hospital for two years before returning to Portugal. He married in August 1970 and, in January 1971, after basic training in Mafra (northwest of Lisbon), left for the colonial war in Angola, where he remained until March 1973. Upon his return to Lisbon, he worked as a poorly paid intern in various hospitals and wrote in his spare time, usually late at night and into the small hours.

The horror, chaos, and injustice that Lobo Antunes experienced as a young medic in Angola left a profound mark on him and became the theme of several of his earlier novels, including this, his second book, for which he found a publisher in 1979, six years after his return from Africa. *Os cus de Judas* (*The Land at the End of the World*) was the first of his books to receive widespread critical acclaim in Portugal and abroad. In 1985—four novels later—Lobo Antunes became a full-time writer, although he continued for many years to treat a few patients at the Hospital Miguel Bombarda—in order, as he said, to persuade himself that he was not mad and, as he put it in another of his novels, to be able to continue "to fish in the agitated, rancorous aquarium of their brains." To date, he has written more than twenty novels and has won innumerable literary prizes in Portugal and elsewhere. His novels tend to be long, seamless, and polyphonic, with many voices jockeying to have their say. Miraculously, out of what can seem at first like an incomprehensible hubbub, there emerge complex characters, a powerful sense of place, and the thread of a gripping story. *The Land at the End of the World* is unusual in having only one narrator and one silent listener, but the many voices are already there, for example, in the aunts' withering comments, the spoof titles of self-help manuals, and his comrades' despairing rants.

The real joy of any Lobo Antunes novel lies in his use of language. The narrator may rail against moral and emotional stagnation, his own and Portugal's, but the prose in which he does this is wildly, surreally restless, constantly broaching new frontiers. He describes his sexual encounter with his anonymous listener as having "all the limp joy of two strands of spaghetti entwining"; a black bra draped over a chair is "like a bat waiting for darkness to come in order to leave its rafter in the attic"; thunder clouds advance "in dark billows toward the barracks, rolling the enormous pianos of the clouds down the stairways of the air"; his mother's knitting needles "secrete" sweaters as they clash "like domesticated fencing foils." This is a book written out of anger and disgust at the folly of war, a war in which Lobo Antunes himself, as a doctor, saw bodies blown apart and mutilated. The experience contaminates the narrator's whole life, the world becomes an ugly, ailing human body. The pink dawn sky is described as being "as empty as the roof of a toothless mouth," the new day grows "as painful and swollen as a boil, sheltering inside it a pus of clocks and tiredness," and his extended similes all too often end in death:

. . . this bathroom is an aquarium of tiles run aground in the water of the night and in which my face moves with the slow, rippling gestures of a sea anemone, my arms wave spasmodically like the boneless farewells of octopuses, while my body is relearning the white immobility of coral. When I lather up my face, Sofia, I can feel the glass scales of my skin on my fingers, my eyes resemble the sad, bulging eyes of the sea bream on the kitchen table, angel fins are sprouting from my armpits. I am dissolving, motionless, in the full bathtub, as I imagine fish do when they die in rivers, evaporating into a sticky foam, their putrefying eyes bobbing about on the surface.

Nothing in this world is clean or simple; it's a zoo, and like the zoo in the opening pages, it is full of strange hybrids:

. . . ostriches that looked just like spinster gym teachers, waddling penguins like messenger boys with bunions, and cockatoos with their heads on one side like connoisseurs of paintings. . . .

Even when these images are comical, they paint a picture of a tainted universe, where almost everything is tarnished by absurdity, bitterness, or grotesquerie. There are exceptions, brief moments of beauty: the harsh splendor of the vast Angolan landscape or its fields of sunflowers; and still briefer moments of loving and of feeling loved: his Aunt Madalena calling him "dear boy" and stroking his hair; his (ex-)wife saying in a tiny, beseeching voice, "Let me kiss you"; and his memory of sitting for hours "exchanging wise, ancient, knowing smiles" with his four-month-old daughter. Those moments, however, are lost in the past; beauty and love do not exist in the present at all.

THE TITLE OF this novel in Portuguese is *Os cus de Judas*, *"cu de Judas"* being a slang term for any very remote, desolate place—"the back of beyond," "the middle of nowhere," "the boonies"—but literally it means "Judas's asshole." It refers here to the godforsaken parts of Angola to which the narrator is drafted as a doctor in the Portuguese army, but it extends, in this contaminated universe, to the Lisbon to which he comes home. There is also perhaps the troubling suggestion that the war in Angola was, as the scholar Luís Madureira has pointed out, a form of colonial sodomy—the Portuguese state simultaneously violating the rebellious colony and its own reluctant, traumatized troops; the sterile reverse of the Portuguese empire's self-image as a virile, fructifying force, a bringer of civilization. The expression *"os cus de Judas"* recurs throughout the novel, where I have translated it as "assholes of the world." However, as a title, that seems too flip, too superficial, lacking as it does the suggestion of treachery in the name "Judas." Another phrase echoes through the novel as well: *"The Land at the End of the World"*

(*As Terras do Fim do Mundo*), which is what Angolans call the remote, back-of-beyond part of Eastern Angola to which Lobo Antunes and his comrades were posted. This name perfectly captures the all-pervading sense of abandonment felt by Portuguese troops and Angolans alike, the sense that they had been swept into a far corner of the world and forgotten, like so much dust and detritus.

The Portuguese Colonial War, as it came to be known, lasted from 1961 to 1974; in its final years, it was serviced by increasingly ill-prepared and bewildered Portuguese conscripts who, like Lobo Antunes himself, were sent off to fight an often-invisible guerrilla enemy in three of Portugal's African colonies: Angola, Mozambique, and Guinea-Bissau. But perhaps we need to go a little farther back in time to see the origins of those wars.

As European nations grappled with their national identity in the calamitous aftermath of the end of World War I and the Treaty of Versailles, Portugal found itself vulnerable to the right-wing forces that were threatening many of Europe's newly created democratic orders. Indeed, the army-led coup on May 28, 1926, against the democratically elected First Republic was the precursor to the authoritarian regime known as the Estado Novo that came into being in 1933. The idea of this "new state" was developed by António de Oliveira Salazar, Portugal's dictatorial prime minister from 1932 to 1968. His pro-Catholic regime—fiercely opposed to Communism, Socialism, and anticolonialism—saw its colonies, entirely erroneously, as a pluricontinental, multiracial empire (other Portuguese colonies were Goa, Macau, and East Timor). Under the Estado Novo, civil liberties and political freedoms were trampled on and censorship was rife; the PIDE, the *Polícia Internacional e de Defesa do Estado* (International and State Defense Police), were instrumental in carrying out the regime's repressive policies in Portugal as well as in the colonies. As the novel suggests, PIDE agents were notorious for their violence and brutality and were greatly feared. The year 1962, however, saw the beginnings of political unrest, with student demonstrations in Lisbon and the formation of independence movements in Angola, Mozambique, and Guinea-Bissau. Lobo Antunes was one of those students, and, when not studying or taking part in demonstrations against the Salazar regime, he was struggling to write his first (never published) novel and discovering writers such as Scott Fitzgerald, Melville, and Faulkner.

In 1968, shortly before Lobo Antunes was shipped to Angola, Salazar suffered a brain hemorrhage and was replaced as prime minister by Marcelo Caetano. Caetano made some minor concessions to the nascent opposition but could not bring himself to stop the colonial wars and give the colonies their independence, despite the accumulating evidence that war was not the solution.

Finally, on April 25, 1974, a group of Portuguese officers, who had formed themselves into the MFA, *Movimento das Forças Armadas* (Armed Forces Movement), overthrew the forty-eight-year-old regime and were greeted in the streets of Lisbon by thousands of jubilant people bearing red carnations. The MFA immediately opened negotiations with the African independence movements; by 1975, Angola, Mozambique, São Tomé e Príncipe, Cape Verde, and Guinea-Bissau were all independent. A new constitution was drawn up, censorship was lifted, and all political prisoners were released. The idealism of those early days of revolution, however, was short-lived. Lobo Antunes himself soon wearied of the speechifying, flag-waving, left-wing ideologues, finding them as repellent as the Fascist ideologues they had replaced and describing their antics as a "a puppet show, a complete farce." Angola and Mozambique, having achieved their hard-won independence, both erupted into violent civil wars that dragged on for more than twenty years. Delirium slid into disillusion and then indifference.

The Land at the End of the World is permeated by those three atmospheres: the years when the narrator was growing up in the repressive, pseudopatriotic society of Salazar's regime; the last bitter, shabby years of the war in Angola; and the immediate post-Revolution years in Portugal. For the narrator, there is no liberation from the horrors he has experienced, no Carnation Revolution. After the vast, empty plains of Angola, Lisbon seems narrow and parochial, and he feels that he belongs nowhere—not in his family, his marriage, his career, or even his own apartment. The chapters follow the alphabet in orderly fashion (the letters *K*, *W*, and *Y* are missing, by the way, because they do not exist in the standard Portuguese alphabet), but that order is, of course, entirely arbitrary. The narrator's experience of the Angolan war has disrupted any order his life may have had, rendering marriage, career, friendships, and family relationships more alphabet soup than alphabet.

An existential horror has entered him like a poison, although, one suspects, the poison of isolation had been there since childhood. As well as being a novel about the futility of war and its dehumanizing effects, *The Land at the End of the World* presents us, too, with a portrait of someone psychologically and emotionally marooned, a man who, like the Ancient Mariner, is driven to tell his story to whoever will listen—in this case, whichever hapless, lonely, desperate female he comes across. His monologue is addressed to a nameless, voiceless woman, who could be any of the various women the narrator has presumably sat next to on any given night in a bar, and with whom he has then gotten drunk and had sex. She doesn't matter; what matters is that he gets to repeat his tale of horrors and to confess to his equivalent of the Ancient Mariner's slain albatross, his cowardice in failing to speak out at the time against the inhumanity and brute stupidity of the war.

The novel was enormously popular in Portugal when it first came out and continues to be read and admired, much as we continue to read the novels and poetry that came out of World Wars I and II and out of the Vietnam debacle, as reminders (if we need them) that we should always question both the morality of war and the wisdom of our leaders' decisions to enter into wars whose horrors they themselves will rarely experience firsthand.

MARGARET JULL COSTA
July 2010

The Land at the End of the World

A

The thing I liked best about the zoo was the roller-skating rink under the trees and the very upright black instructor describing slow ellipses as he glided effortlessly backward over the concrete surface, surrounded by girls in short skirts and white boots, who, if they spoke, doubtless did so in the same gauzy tones as those voices you hear at airports announcing the departure of planes, cotton syllables that dissolve in the ear just as the remnants of a piece of candy do on the curled shell of the tongue. I know it may sound idiotic, but, on Sunday mornings, when we used to visit the zoo with my father, the animals seemed more real somehow, the lofty, long-drawn-out solitude of the giraffe resembled that of a glum Gulliver, and from the headstones in the dog cemetery there arose, from time to time, the mournful howls of poodles. The zoo had a whiff about it like the open-air passageways in the Coliseu concert hall, a place full of strange invented birds in cages, ostriches that looked just like spinster gym teachers, waddling penguins like messenger boys with bunions, and cockatoos with their heads on one side like connoisseurs of paintings; the hippopotamus pool exuded the languid sloth of the obese, cobras lay coiled in soft dungy spirals, and the crocodiles seemed reconciled to their Tertiary-age fate as mere lizards on death row. The plane trees between the cages were turning gray like us, and it seemed to me that we were, in a way, growing old together: the attendant raking leaves into a bucket bore a strange resemblance to the surgeon who, years later, would sweep my gallstones into an open bottle bearing a sticky label; a vegetable menopause, in which the lumps in the prostate and the knots on the tree trunks merged and blended, would unite us, like brothers, in the same illusionless melancholy; molars would fall from the mouth like rotten fruit, the skin on our bellies would hang in rough, husklike folds. And it was not impossible that a conspiratorial breath would shake the locks of our hair on the highest branches, and that a banal cough would penetrate the mist of deafness like the bellowing of a conch shell, which would gradually take on the soothing tones of a bout of conjugal catarrh.

The zoo's restaurant—where the smell of animals wafted in dilute scraps into the steaming stew, adding to the potatoes an unpleasant hint of bristle and to the meat the fibrous texture of carpet—was usually full, in equal quantities, of parties of daytrippers and impatient mothers, who shooed away with their forks balloons that drifted about like absentminded smiles trailing bits of twine behind them, like a Chagall bride trailing the hem of her dress. Elderly ladies dressed in blue, with trays of cakes resting on their bellies, proffered custard cream puffs as powdery as their own puff-pastry cheeks under siege from stickily persistent flies. Skeletal dogs, straight out of some medieval painting, hesitated between receiving a swift kick from the waiters and snaffling the sausages that dangled from the plates to the floor like superfluous fingers shiny with the brilliantine of oil. The paddleboats on the lake threatened, at any moment, to sail straight through the open windows and bob about on the hostile waves of paper napkins. And outside, indifferent to the lusterless music made duller still by the loudspeakers, to the ox's mournful laments, to the day-trippers' jollity, like the weary rattle of tambourines, and to my own mingled excitement, admiration, and wonder, the black instructor continued to slide motionlessly around that rink beneath the trees with the rare and marvelous majesty of a litter being carried backward.

If, for example, you and I were anteaters, rather than two people sitting in the corner of a bar, I might feel more comfortable with your silence, with your motionless hands holding your glass, with your glazed fish eyes fixing now on my balding head and now on my navel, we might be able to understand each other better in a meeting of restless snouts sniffing halfheartedly at the concrete for nonexistent insects, we might come together, under cover of darkness, in acts of sexual coitus as sad as Lisbon nights, when the Neptunes in the lakes slough off the mud and slime and scan the deserted squares with blank, eager, rust-colored eyes. Perhaps you would finally tell me about yourself. Perhaps behind your Cranach brow there lies sleeping a secret fondness for rhinoceroses. Perhaps, if you felt my body, you would discover that I had been suddenly transformed into a unicorn, and I would embrace you, and you would flap startled arms, like a butterfly transfixed by a pin, your voice grown husky with desire. We would buy tickets for the train that travels around the zoo, from creature to creature, with its clockwork engine, an escapee from some provincial haunted castle, and we would wave, as we passed, at the grotto-cum-crib of those recycled carpets—the polar bears. We would observe with an ophthalmological eye the baboons' anal conjunctivitis, like eyelids inflamed with combustible hemorrhoids. We would kiss outside the lions' den, where the lions—moth-eaten old overcoats—would curl their lips to reveal toothless gums. I would stroke your breasts in the oblique shade cast by the foxes, you would buy me an ice cream on a stick from the clowns' enclosure, where they, eyebrows permanently arched, exchanged blows to the tragic accompaniment of a saxophone. And that way we would have recovered a little of the childhood that belongs to neither of us and that insists on whizzing down the children's slide with a laugh that reaches us now as an occasional faint, almost angry echo.

Do you remember the stone eagles at the entrance to the zoo and the ticket offices like sentry boxes where musty employees officiated, blinking myopic owl eyes in the damp gloom? My parents lived not far away, near a shop selling coffins and doing a mystic trade in wax hands and busts of Father Cruz,* which, at night, whenever the tigers roared, shuddered on their shelves in arthritic terror, cripples ready to adorn dainty oval doilies on the tops of refrigerators, whose frigorific purrings then seemed to emanate from the invalids' own clay esophaguses, as if they were struggling to digest one too many cookies. From my brothers' bedroom window, you could see the camels, whose expression of profound boredom lacked only a fat managerial cigar to complete the look. Seated on the toilet, where the final remnant of a river in its death agony uttered intestinal gurglings, you could hear the laments of the seals, whose excessive girth prevented them from swimming down the pipes and out through the taps, grunting like impatient math examiners. On certain nights—in a commerce that has

---

*Father Francisco Rodrigues da Cruz (1859–1948) was a Portuguese priest who traveled throughout Portugal helping the poor and those in prisons and hospitals. His name was put forward for beatification in 1951.

remained inflation-proof over the centuries—my mother's bed would creak in response to the dictates of my father's asthmatic panting, to the rhythmic urgings of her mahout, making a noise like the toothless, lumbago-ridden elephant clanging its bell to get its daily ration of cabbage.

The woman who sold almonds, and whose left elbow was missing, set up her baskets beneath our balcony and regaled my grandmother with long tales of her husband's violent drinking bouts, worthy of several chapters by Maxim Gorky. The mornings filled up with toucans and ibises fed on the crumbs from the breakfast rolls that left flour on our fingers, like dust from the furniture. A spot of afternoon sunlight trotted across the floor with the furtive step of a hyena, alternately revealing and concealing the successive designs on the carpet, the chipped baseboard, the photo hanging on the wall of our fireman uncle, resplendent with mustache, whose polished helmet had the domestic gleam of a brass doorknob. In the hall was a beveled mirror, which, at night, emptied of images, became as deep as the eyes of a sleeping baby, capable of containing both the trees in the zoo and the orangutans hanging from their metal rings like enormous frozen spiders. At the time, I nursed the absurd hope that, one day, I would trace graceful spirals around the black instructor's majestic hyperbolas, wearing white boots and pink trousers, gliding along to the sound of pulleys that I always imagined must have accompanied the precarious flight of Giotto's angels, swinging through biblical skies on innocent invisible wires. The trees surrounding the skating rink would close behind me, intertwining their dense shadows, and that would be my way of leaving. Perhaps when I'm old and reduced to living with my clocks and my cats in a third-floor apartment with no elevator, my disappearance will be seen not as that of a shipwreck victim drowning among boxes of pills and poultices, herbal teas and prayers to the Holy Spirit, but of the boy who will rise up from me, like the soul from the body in those engravings in the catechism, in order to pirouette unsteadily toward the very upright black instructor, his hair slicked down with gloss and his lips curved to form the enigmatic and infinitely indulgent smile of a Buddha on roller skates.

In my mind, that guardian-angel-in-a-tie replaced forever the virtuous postcard of Sãozinha* with her suspiciously plump cheeks that made her look like some Mae West of the sacristy deep in mystical love with a Christ sporting a thin Douglas Fairbanks mustache in the silent cinema of my aunts' chapel, for my aunts all lived in large dark houses, in which the bas reliefs of the sofas and other furniture only thickened the gloom and where the keys of the pianos, draped in damask shawls, showed their glittering, decaying teeth. Every building in Rua Barata Salgueiro, sad as a rainy recess at school, was inhabited by some aged relative rowing with a walking stick down a river of carpets replete with Chinese vases and inlaid chests of drawers that a tide of generations of goateed traders had abandoned there as if it were the final beach. The houses smelled of stale air, influenza, and cookies, and only the large, rusty bathtubs, with their clawed sphinx's feet and the line of absent water indicated by a brown rim similar to the mark left on the head by a hat, only they seemed alive to me, their vast throats hungry for the faucets' copper tits, from which there fell, from time to time,

---

* Maria da Conceição Ferrão de Pimentel (1923–1940), known as Sãozinha, was a brilliant student at school and very pious. Her one sadness was that her father was an unbeliever. At the age of eighteen, she offered up her own life in exchange for her father's conversion. She died two months later. Her father converted a month after her death.

strange tears like drops of Argyrol. In all the kitchens, which resembled the chemistry labs at school, there would be a missionary calendar on the wall full of pictures of pickaninnies, and an ageless maid, inevitably named Albertina, would be preparing chicken broth with no salt and muttering her prayers over the pots to season the white rice. In the ancient boilers, as old as Papin's* steam engine, gas flames flickered like fragile petals, wavering on the verge of a catastrophic explosion that would reduce every last Sèvres teacup to unrecognizable smithereens. The windows were indistinguishable from the paintings: through the glass and on canvas one saw, adorned with the faded streamers of a defunct Carnival, the same October trees, as shriveled as a child's willy after a dip in a particularly cold swimming pool. The aunts would lurch toward me like dancers on music boxes when the clockwork was about to wind down, then point the quavering threat of their walking sticks at my ribs, scornfully eye the padding in my jacket, and declare sourly, You're awfully thin, as if my prominent clavicles were more shameful than a smear of lipstick on my collar.

A pendulum clock, lost somewhere among the dark cupboards, chimed the muffled hours in some distant corridor crammed with camphor chests and leading to stiff, damp bedrooms, in which the corpse of Proust still floated, filling the rarefied air with a breath burnished with childhood. My aunts installed themselves with some difficulty on the edges of vast armchairs decorated with crocheted filigrees, poured tea from teapots as elaborately worked as

*Denis Papin (1647–1712) was a French-born British physicist who invented the pressure cooker and whose design for the first cylinder-and-piston steam engine, though impractical, led to development of the first effective steam engine.

Manueline* monstrances, and completed their ejaculatory prayers by pointing with the sugar spoon at photographs of irate generals—who had died before I was born and after waging glorious battle over backgammon and billiards in mess halls as melancholy as empty dining rooms—and of Last Suppers that had been replaced by engravings of battlefields.

"At least doing his military service will make a man of him."

This vigorous prophecy, uttered throughout my childhood and adolescence by false teeth of indisputable authority, continued to be delivered in strident tones at the canasta tables, where the females of the clan provided a pagan counterweight to Sunday Mass at two *centavos* a point, a nominal sum that served as a way of venting, by playing the winning card, ancient enmities patiently secreted over the years. The men of the family, whose pompous solemnity had fascinated me before I was of an age to make my First Communion, when I had not yet realized that their whispered confabulations, as inaccessible and vital as the gatherings of gods, were about the merits of the maid's eminently pinchable bottom, all lent their earnest support to my aunts with the intention of removing a possible future rival when it came to dealing out furtive pinches as the table was being cleared. The specter of Salazar hovered over their pious bald pates like the diminutive flames of some corporate Holy Spirit, keeping us safe from the dark and dangerous idea of Socialism. The PIDE courageously continued their valiant crusade against the sinister notion of democracy, which would, of course, be a first step toward our silver cutlery disappearing into the greedy pockets of

---

*The Manueline style is also known as Portuguese late Gothic, a particularly ornate style of architectural ornamentation prevalent in Portugal in the first decades of the sixteenth century.

newspaper vendors and apprentices. The framed photo of Cardinal Cerejeira* guaranteed, on the one hand, the continuance of the Society of St. Vincent de Paul and, by extension, of the tamed and mastered poor. The picture of the rabble gathered around a libertarian guillotine and howling with joy had been sent into permanent exile in the attic, along with old bidets and three-legged chairs, which a dusty chink of sunlight bathed in the kind of mystery that only emphasizes the futility of all abandoned objects. And so when I embarked for Angola, on board a ship packed with soldiers, in order finally to become a man, the tribe, grateful to the Government for making such a metamorphosis possible and at no expense to them, turned up in force on the quayside, putting up, in a moment of patriotic fervor, with being elbowed by an excited and anonymous crowd, very similar to the one in the picture showing the guillotine, gathered there as impotent witnesses to their own deaths.

* Manuel Gonçalves Cerejeira was appointed cardinal when he was only forty-two. He was a close friend and ally of Salazar and a supporter of the Estado Novo.

B

Do you know the military base at Santa Margarida? I ask because, sometimes, in the officers' mess—decorated with the stubbornly impersonal bad taste of a dentist's waiting room in Moscavide (plastic flowers, vague oleographs whose monotonous arabesques blend with the wallpaper, and stiff-backed chairs like unmatched pairs of quadrupeds randomly grazing the worn fringes of rugs)—the rowdy majors would put down their glasses of whisky, with poker dice for ice cubes, and stand to attention like paunchy tin soldiers to greet the entrance of a lady convoyed in by some suddenly urbane colonel, an event that set the gold braid trembling and left behind it a whispered trail of soldierly lust that would later find expression in explanatory drawings on the veined marble of the urinals, intended, naturally, for the elucidation of illiterate cleaning ladies.

Masturbation was our daily workout, we were pistons huddled in our icy sheets like aged fetuses no uterus would ever expel, while outside, the pine trees and the fog met in an inextricable tangle of damp murmurings, with the trees superimposing on the night the sticky dark of their trunks, sugared by the mist's fairground cotton candy. It was like being a child again visiting the seaside at Praia das Maçãs in late September, and going to bed and feeling that your body was a tiny seed lost in the vast, rumpled, tremulous mattress, the hairs on your arms and legs bristling in alarm at the sound of the sea below, which seemed to come from nowhere, reaching out and drawing back, like the gravelly bronchitis of invisible lungs. Cuckoo clocks gave way to the equally irritating sound of bugles, uniform and skin converged to form a single military carapace, the shaven heads and the parades reminded me of the summer camps of my youth with their sickly sweet smell of unwashed bodies and that sense of slightly indignant resignation. On Sundays, the whole rejoicing family came to check on the progress of that metamorphosis from civilian larva into perfect warrior, with beret glued firmly on head like a capsule and gigantic boots covered in the historic mud of Verdun, halfway between mythomaniac Scout and unknown Carnival soldier. And all of this took place in a kind of boarding-school atmosphere that the barracks subtly prolonged, with its secrets, its initiation ceremonies, its childishly perverse stratagems intended to elude the vigilance of the prefects—our commanding officers—who were more concerned with winning at bridge, on which would depend the smooth or difficult digestion of their evening meal, than with any nocturnal shenanigans in the barracks rooms hidden away beneath the musty scurf dropped by the plane trees, where skinny dogs, like El Greco greyhounds, joined in melancholy coitus and fixed us with the painfully imploring eyes of dying nuns.

In Mafra, beneath the rain, I watched the mice scampering about between the bunks in the monastery's boundless gloom, a labyrinth of corridors haunted by the ghosts of quartermasters. In Tomar, where the fish emerge from the River Mouchão and swim aimlessly along the streets in scintillating shoals, I made matchstick models of the Monastery of the Jerónimos, to the yellow-eyed amazement of jaundiced parachutists. In Elvas, side by side with a fat recruit as wobbly as a crème caramel on a plate, I longed to disappear through the city walls just as Chagall's violinists merge with the dense blue of the canvas, and, flapping the clumsy cotton wings of my military sleeves, come to rest in Paris where I would live a revolutionary's exile composed of abstract paintings and concrete poems, for which the *Diário de Notícias* in the Casa de Portugal would supply the necessary Lusitanian ballast of wedding announcements—chaste as farsighted notaries—and notices of seventh-day Masses sweetened by the disembodied smiles of the dead. And in Santa Margarida, waiting for the boat, I herded long lines of soldiers toward a demented dentist who depopulated gums, howling with murderous glee as he did so.

"At least you won't have any problems with these guys getting toothaches," he roared at me, bent over his ghastly dentist's chair, aglow with satisfaction and sweat, thrusting the flaming blowtorch of his drill into another terrified jaw.

The ladies from the National Women's Movement would visit occasionally to give their menopausal mink coats an outing by distributing Our Lady of Fátima medals and key rings bearing the image of Salazar, both of which came accompanied by nationalistic Our Fathers and threats of biblical hell in the prison at Peniche, where the PIDE agents did a far better job than the innocent pitchfork-wielding devils of the catechism. I always imagined the ladies' pubic hair to be like a fox-fur stole and thought that, when aroused, drops of Ma Griffe and poodle drool would dribble from their vaginas, leaving shiny snail trails on their wrinkled thighs. Seated at the brigadier's table, they sipped their soup with cautiously pursed lips, rather as hemorrhoid sufferers lower themselves gingerly onto the edges of sofas, and on their paper napkins they left heart-shaped lipstick traces that spoke of quarrels with maids and remnants of patriotic tirades, and on the morning of our departure, I met them again on the ship's gangway, encouraging us with packs of Três Vintes cigarettes and manly handshakes from hands with knuckles like signet rings.

"Don't you worry, we in the rearguard will remain vigilant."

Indeed, when one thought about it, there was little to fear from such sad, drooping buttocks, in relation to which the waist made do with the secondary role of truss.

And then, well, you know how it is, Lisbon began to move away from me in an ever-fainter tumult of martial music above whose chords fluttered the usual tragic, immobile faces of farewell, which memory freezes into expressions of horror. The mirror in my cabin reflected back at me features dislocated by anxiety, like a jigsaw puzzle in pieces, in which the pained grimace of a smile took on the repellent sinuosity of a scar. One of the doctors was bent over his bunk, his whole body shaken by convulsive sobs, like the irregular palpitations of a stuttering taxi, the other was studying his fingers with the vacant interest of newborn babes or of idiots who spend hours, eyes rapt, licking their own nails, and I was asking myself just what we were doing there, in that state of suspended death, on the throbbing sewing-machine deck of the ship, with Lisbon drowning in the distance and uttering one last hymnal sigh. Suddenly bereft of a past, with the Salazar key ring and the Fátima medal in my pocket, and standing between the dollhouse-size bathtub and washbasin riveted to the wall, I felt like my parents' house in summer, with no curtains, rugs rolled up in newspaper, furniture pushed into the corners and covered in large dusty shrouds, the silver relegated to my grandmother's pantry, and the gigantic echo of no one's footsteps in the empty rooms. It's like when you cough in an underground parking lot at night, I thought, and you feel the unbearable weight of your own solitude in your ears, in the form of a thunderous thudding, identical to the beating of your temples on the drum of your pillow.

On the second day, we reached Madeira, a fruit cake decorated with crystallized houses floating on the blue china tray of the sea, Alenquer* adrift on the silence of the afternoon. The ship's orchestra blasted out boleros for the officers, who looked as melancholy as owls caught in the dawn light, and from the hold, where the soldiers were all crammed together, rose a thick exhalation of vomit, a smell I had completely forgotten from the far-off noontides of childhood, when, in the kitchen, at lunchtime, my reluctant soup bowl would be surrounded by the faces of my family, their expressions alternately encouraging and threatening, with each spoonful I swallowed underlined by a round of bright applause, until someone paying proper attention cried:

"Sing him a song, he's going to be sick."

In response to this terrible warning, all the adults burst into discordant unison as if they were standing on the deck of the sinking *Titanic*, lips curled back over their gold teeth, while a maid kept time with saucepan lids, the gardener shouldered a broom and pretended to march, and I fetched up a confusion of pasta and rice that they then forced me to eat again, accompanied this time not by singing but by the angry hiss of insults. And so, you see, reclining in a deck chair and sensing in my increasingly sweaty collar the implacable metamorphosis of Lisbon winter into gelatinous equa-

---

* Alenquer is an attractive small town just north of Lisbon.

torial summer, as soft and warm on my neck as the hands of Senhor Melo, my grandfather's barber, in his shop in Rua 1º de Dezembro, where the moist air multiplied the chrome glitter of scissors in the reverse world of the mirrors, what I most fervently wanted then was for Gija, as she used to do in those long-lost days, to come and rub my thin, small-boy's ribs in a gesture that was both patient and tender, until I fell asleep and dreamed dreams conjured up by the soothing rake of her fingers that could drive out of my body the desperate or frightened ghosts that inhabit it.

C

―――――――――

My first impression of Luanda was of a shabby harbor without a hint of majesty, its warehouses shimmering in the humidity and heat. The water resembled murky sun lotion smeared onto old, grubby skin veined with rotting cables. Squatting in small groups, black men—blurred figures in the brilliant, tremulous light—were watching us with the timeless absorption, simultaneously acute and blind, that you see in photographs showing the closed, inward-turned eyes of John Coltrane as he played his bittersweet, drunken-angel music on the saxophone, and I imagined, before the thick lips of each of those men, an invisible trumpet about to rise vertically in the dense air like a fakir's rope. Thin white birds dissolved into the palm trees around the bay or into the wooden houses far off on Luanda Island, thick with trees and insects, where whores, worn out by heartless men from Lisbon, went to drink one last glass of champagne soda, like dying whales stranded on a final beach, occasionally jiggling their hips to the *pasodoble* beat of some indecipherable anxiety. Tiny bespectacled second lieutenants, with the competent air of scrupulous student workers, shepherded us smartly in the direction of cattle trucks waiting on a pier covered in detritus and slime, like the pier at Cruz Quebrada, where the sewers lie dying at Lisbon's feet and elderly dogs vomit up garbage: wherever we Portuguese go in the world, we mark our adventurous presence with ornate Manueline designs and empty tin cans, a subtle combination of heroic scurvy and rusty tinplate. I've always been in favor of erecting in some suitable square in Portugal a monument to spit, a spitting bust, a spitting marshal, a spitting poet, a spitting statesman, a spitting equestrian statue, something that would provide, in the future, a perfect definition of the perfect Portuguese male: someone who spits and boasts about his sexual prowess. As for philosophy, my dear friend, we need only consult the newspaper editorials, about as rich in ideas as the Gobi Desert is in Eskimos, so much so that our brains grow weary with their complicated arguments and require us to drink vials of some special elixir, to be taken at mealtimes, to help us think.

Do you fancy another Drambuie? Talking about elixirs always makes me long for syrupy, amber-yellow liquids in the vain hope that, through them and the gentle, cheerful dizziness they provoke, I might discover the secret of life and of people, an emotional squaring of the circle. Sometimes, by the sixth or seventh glass, I feel that I'm almost there, that I'm about to grasp it, that the clumsy tweezers of my understanding are about to pick up, with surgical caution, the delicate nucleus of the mystery, but then I immediately sink into the formless glee of inarticulate idiocy from which I only extricate myself the following day, by dint of aspirin and antacids, stumbling over my slippers on the way to work, carrying with me the hopeless opacity of my existence, as thick with the mud of enigmas as the half-dissolved sugar in my morning cup of coffee. Has the same thing never happened to you, have you never felt that you were so close that, at any moment, you were going to achieve a long-postponed and eternally pursued ambition, the project that is both your despair and your hope, have you never, with a feeling of uncontrollable joy, reached out to grasp that thing only to fall flat on your back, your fingers closed around nothing, while the ambition or the project or whatever trotted calmly and indifferently away, without so much as a backward glance? But perhaps you've never experienced that horrific sense of defeat, perhaps for you metaphysics is merely an inconvenience as ephemeral as a passing itch, perhaps you possess the gleeful lightness of a moored boat, bobbing slowly about like some autonomously rocking cradle. In fact, one of the things I find so charming about you, if you'll allow me to say so, is your innocence, not the innocent innocence of children or the police, composed of a kind of inner virginity acquired at the expense of credulity or stupidity, but the wise, resigned, almost vegetable innocence of those who expect of others and themselves precisely what you and I, sitting here, expect of the barman whom I summon by raising my arm like some chronically keen student, namely, a vague, distracted attentiveness and an utter disdain for the measly tip of our gratitude.

Crammed with suitcases and the timid dread felt by all foreigners in another land, whose strangely Lusitanian qualities seemed to us as unlikely as an honest government minister, the train finally waddled like a pouter pigeon out of the port and headed for Luanda's poor suburbs. The colorful squalor of the slums around Luanda, the slow thighs of the women, the fat starvation bellies of the children, who sat motionless on the banks, watching us, or else dragged along behind them some pathetic toy on a string, began to awaken in me a strange sense of the absurd that had been nagging me ever since we left Lisbon, in my head or in my guts, in the physical guise of some unlocatable affliction, an affliction apparently shared by one of the priests on board, who had grown weary of finding in his breviary biblical justifications for massacres of innocents. We met sometimes at night, at the ship's rail, he clasping a book and I with my hands in my pockets, both of us staring out at the same black, opaque waves on which reflections (from what lights? from what stars? from what vast pupils?) sometimes leaped like fish, as if we were both seeking in that dark horizontal expanse plowed by the ship's propellers some enlightening response to our unformulated disquiets. I lost sight of that priest (indeed, I seem fated to lose sight all too quickly of all the priests and all the women I meet), but I recall with the clarity of a childhood nightmare the look on his face, like that of a puzzled Noah forced to set sail in an ark full of creatures with colic, dragged from the native forests of their government offices, billiard tables, and clubs, and catapulted, in the name of vehemently held but imbecilic ideas, into two years of anguish, uncertainty, and death. There could be no doubt about the truth of the latter: large coffins complete with biers occupied one part of the hold, and we used to play a somewhat macabre game that consisted of trying to guess, by studying the faces of the other men and our own, who the coffins' future occupants would be. Him? Me? Both of us? Or the fat major over there talking to the second lieutenant in charge of radio communications? Whenever you examine people closely, they begin, imperceptibly, to take on not so much a familiar aspect but a kind of posthumous profile, which we dignify with our fantasy about their future disappearance. Fondness, friendship, even a degree of tenderness all become easier, being pleasant comes effortlessly, idiocy takes on the amiably seductive quality of ingenuousness. Deep down, of course, it is our own death that we fear when we imagine someone else's—and that is what makes cowards of us all.

What about switching to vodka? One can face the specter of death better with tongue and stomach on fire, and any kind of alcohol that tastes of lamp oil, and smells like the kind of perfume some great-aunt might wear, has the beneficent virtue of setting off my gastritis and, as a consequence, making me braver: there's nothing like heartburn to dissolve fear or, if you prefer, to transform one's usual passive egotism into a state of impetuous agitation, not so very different in essence, but more active: Napoleon's famous ulcer, you may remember, was the secret key to his victories at Wagram and Austerlitz. And these saucers full of small, poisonous, salted things, which I'm sure the emperor never tasted, will pass through our intestines like grains of lye and prove capable of hurling us, thanks to a touch of colic, into the maddest or sweetest of adventures. Perhaps, who knows, you and I will end the night making love to one another, as furiously as rhinoceroses with toothaches, until the morning sheds its pale light on sheets disheveled by our desperate ruttings. The astonished neighbors in the apartment below will imagine that I've brought home two pachyderms intent on devouring each other amid a concert of squeals, half loathing, half birth pangs, and perhaps, who knows, this novelty will arouse in them long-dormant feelings and cause them to lock together like the pieces of one of those Japanese puzzles impossible to pull apart except with the infinite patience of a surgeon or the expeditious knife of a professional gelder. Are you capable of bringing me breakfast in bed, smelling already of toothpaste and optimism? Of whistling through your teeth as bakers used to do, floury angels with a basket slung over one shoulder who took the place of those weary owls, the night watchmen, and who constitute one of the less melancholy segments of my childhood memories? Are you capable of loving? Sorry, that's a stupid question, because all women are capable of loving and those who aren't love themselves through others, which, in practice, and at least for the first few months, is almost indistinguishable from genuine affection. Take no notice of me, the wine is having its usual effect and, any moment now, I'll be asking you to marry me: that's what tends to happen. When I'm feeling very alone or when I've drunk too much, a little wax bouquet of conjugality starts to sprout inside me the way mold grows inside locked cupboards, and I become clinging, vulnerable, maudlin, and totally feeble; that, I warn you now, is the moment to sneak off, making some excuse or other, and get into your car with a sigh of relief, and call your friends from the hairdresser's, telling them, with a snicker, about my unimaginative propositions. Meanwhile, if you don't mind, until that time comes, I'll bring my chair a little closer and have another drink or two with you.

The train that fled with us from that African Cruz Quebrada and from its crown of rusting cranes and long-legged gulls finally deposited us in a kind of barracks in the far-flung outskirts of Luanda, concrete blocks burning up in the heat, where the sweat crackled and boiled on your skin. In the officers' quarters, surrounded by banana trees with large fringed leaves, like the wings of decaying archangels, the mosquitoes penetrated the netting covering the windows and, in the dark, kept up a shrill, insistent hum in which my blood sang, free of me at last, sucked out in swift mouthfuls. Outside, I was surprised by a sky of unfamiliar stars and was sometimes assailed by the feeling that someone had superimposed a false universe on the one I was used to, and that I would simply have to peel away that strange, fragile scenery to return to my normal, day-to-day world, one peopled with familiar faces and smells that accompanied me as faithfully as dogs. We dined in the city on sordid esplanades packed with soldiers, where miserable bootblacks shuffled, squatting, from one set of knees to another, casting passionately vehement glances at our boots, and where legless individuals timidly proffered fetishes carved with a penknife, the equivalent of those plastic models of the Torre de Belém you can buy in Lisbon. Greasy white guys, briefcase under one arm, changed Portuguese money for Angolan money with the knowing languor of practiced moneylenders; streets, every one identical to Rua Morais Soares in Lisbon, approached and moved off in a tangled labyrinth en route to the fort, and the avenues were sprinkled with blinking, squinting orange pools of provincial neon lights. Anchored in the bay, the ship that had brought us lay mirrored in the water where it was preparing to depart: it would return without me to the winter and the fog of Lisbon, where everything, irritatingly, would carry on in my absence in the usual way, causing me to think resentfully about what would inevitably happen after my death, and which would, after all, be only the prolongation of the lukewarm, neutral indifference that I knew so well, unmarked by either enthusiasm or tragedy and composed of days tacked one onto the other in a glum bureaucracy free of any burning anxieties. Do you believe in upheavals, great adventures, inner earthquakes, soaring flights of ecstasy? Forget it, my friend, it's nothing but an optical illusion, smoke and mirrors, a mere theatrical trick no more real than the cardboard and cellophane of the scenery used to create it or the force of our own desire to give it the appearance of movement. Like this bar and its Art Nouveau lamps in dubious taste, its customers, heads together, whispering delicious banalities, caught up in the sweet euphoria of alcohol, the background music lending to our smiles the mysterious depth of feelings we have never had: another half bottle of wine and we'll think ourselves Vermeer, as skilled as he was at translating, through the domestic simplicity of a gesture, the touching, inexpressible bitterness of our condition. The proximity of death makes us warier or, at least, more prudent: in Luanda, while we waited to be dispatched at a moment's notice to the combat zone, we gladly exchanged metaphysics for the tawdry cabarets on Luanda Island, with a whore on either arm, a bucket of cheap champagne on the table, and, on stage, the little squint-eyed striptease artiste taking off her clothes with all the bored indifference of an old snake sloughing off its skin. I sometimes woke up in the rooms of some seedy boardinghouse unable to remember how I had gotten there, and I would pull on my clothes in silence, fumbling for my shoes beneath a discarded black-lace bra, not wanting to disturb the sleep of the vague shape between the sheets, and of whom I could make out only a tangle of hair. True to the family prophecy, I had become a man: a kind of sad, cynical greed made up of lascivious despair, egotism, and an eagerness to hide from myself had replaced forever the fragile pleasure of childish joy, of open, unreserved laughter, embalmed in purity, and which at night, when I'm walking home down a deserted street, I still seem to hear echoing at my back like a mocking cascade.

D

———

*N*o, I'm not in any pain, although my head does ache a little, but it's nothing, a feeling, a touch of dizziness. The monotonous buzz of talk, the mingled smells, the way faces shift and rearrange themselves in the act of speaking, make me giddy: I don't know anyone here, I rarely frequent these exotic temples where people no longer sacrifice the entrails of animals but their own livers, these modern catacombs given a kind of sacrilegious religious feel by the votive lamps of strange lights and the prayerful murmur of conversation, and where the barman is the golden calf, motionless behind the high altar of the bars, surrounded by the deacons or habitués, who raise a ritual glass of black velvet in his honor. Thymol crosses stand in for crucifixes, we fast at Easter in order to lower our cholesterol levels, on Sundays our Holy Communion wafers take the form of detox vitamins, we confess our infidelities to our group analyst, and our penance is his monthly bill: as you see, nothing has changed, except that now we consider ourselves to be atheists because, instead of beating our breast, the doctor does this for us with the end of his stethoscope. Here, I feel like my father used to when he was a child and had to attend Masses held for family members who had died and at which he invariably arrived late, when the Mass was half over, and then he would be made to stand next to the holy-water font, hands behind his back, a duffle-coated Robespierre defying the alms boxes and the sad stone eyes of the saints. I obviously belong somewhere else, I don't know where, but probably somewhere so far back in time and space that I will never again be able to retrieve it, perhaps I belong to the zoo as it once was and to the black instructor gliding backward across the rink beneath the trees, accompanied by the shrieks of the animals and the bell rung by the ice-cream salesman. If I were a giraffe, I would love you in silence, gazing down at you from over the wire fencing, as melancholy as a dockyard crane, I would love you with the awkward love of the very tall, and, thoughtfully chewing a leaf as if it were gum, jealous of the bears, the anteaters, the duck-billed platypuses, the cockatoos, and the crocodiles, I would slowly lower my neck on the pulleys of my tendons in order, tenderly, tremulously, to nuzzle your breasts with my head. Because, and I tell you this in confidence, I am a tender soul, very tender, even before I've had my sixth neat Jim Beam or my eighth Drambuie, I am as stupidly, submissively tender as a sick dog, one of those dogs with imploring, all-too-human eyes, which, from time to time, and for no reason, presses its snout to your heels, whining with all the tormented passion of a slave, and which you end up shooing away with a kick, sending the creature slinking off, doubtless sobbing soppy sonnets and weeping tears of faded violets. There are two things, my dear friend, that I continue to share with the social class from which I come, much to the chagrin of Che Guevara, that Carlos Gardel* of the Revolution, whose poster I pinned above my bed

* Carlos Gardel (1887/1890–1935) is considered to have been the greatest writer and performer of tangos. He died tragically young in an airplane crash.

to protect me from bourgeois nightmares, like a magnetic bracelet of the soul: an awful sentimentalism that makes me snivel whenever I watch a soap opera on the TV in the local bar and a terrible fear of looking ridiculous. For example, I would like, without ostentation or embarrassment, to wear a Tyrolean hat complete with feather to cover my incipient bald patch. Or to let the nail on one little finger grow long. Or to fold up my tram ticket and tuck it under my wedding ring. Or to wear a poor clown's outfit when I see my patients. Or to give you my photo in a heart-shaped enamel frame so that you can look at it when you're fat, because you will be fat one day, believe me, we will all be fat, fat, fat and as placid as neutered cats, while we wait for death at cinema matinees.

However, at the time I'm telling you about, I had hair, a lot of hair, well, a fair bit, although regularly trimmed and hidden beneath my military beret, and I was traveling south from Luanda to Nova Lisboa, in the direction of the war, through a landscape of unbelievably vast horizons. I come from an old, narrow country, you see, from a city suffocating in houses that multiply and reflect each other in their tiled façades and in oval ponds, and the illusion of space I am familiar with here, the sky being blocked with low clouds of pigeons, consists of a scrawny strip of river squeezed between the sharp edges of two corners of land, and across which, in a heroic impulse, a bronze navigator reaches one oblique arm. I was born and grew up in a stunted, crocheted universe, intricate great-aunt–style crochet, they filigreed my head when I was a child, got me used to a kind of bibelot smallness of mind, forbade me to read the rather raunchy ninth canto of *The Lusiads*,* and taught me

---

* The epic poem written by Portugal's national poet, Luís de Camões (c. 1524–1580). It charts, in Homeric fashion, the Portuguese discoveries of the fifteenth and sixteenth centuries.

always to wave my handkerchief instead of simply leaving. In short, they policed my intellect and reduced geography to a mere matter of time zones, to the hourly calculations of a clerk whose caravel bound for the Indies metamorphosed into a Formica table with a sponge on top with which to wet stamps and tongue. Have you ever sat daydreaming, your elbows resting on one of those horrible tables, only to end the day in a third-floor apartment in some dull district like Campo de Ourique or Póvoa de Santo Adrião and spend vacant evenings listening to your own beard growing? Have you ever suffered the daily death of waking up beside someone you mildly detest? Driving to work together, eyes still shadowy with sleep, both of you already heavy with disappointment and tiredness, empty of words, feelings, life? Well, imagine that, suddenly, without warning, the whole of this world in miniature, this whole web of sad habits, this oppressive melancholy the size of a paperweight inside which it's snowing monotonously on and on, imagine that it evaporated, vanished, broke, along with the roots binding it to that quaint embroidered-cushion life of resignation and the links that chained it to people who bored you silly, and you woke up in a truck, not very comfortable, it's true, and, yes, full of soldiers, but driving through an unimaginable landscape, where everything fluctuates—colors, trees, the gigantic shapes of things—and where the sky builds and demolishes stairways of clouds on which your eyes stumble and fall back, like a great enraptured bird.

From time to time, though, Portugal would reappear in the form of small settlements by the roadside, in which the few white inhabitants, translucent with malaria, were desperately trying to re-create lost Lisbon suburbia by hanging ceramic swallows on the wall between the windows or putting up wrought-iron lanterns by the front door; any race that has spent centuries sowing churches inevitably, instinctively ends up adorning the tops of fridges with vases full of plastic flowers, just as Tolstoy, as he lay dying, moved his blind fingers over the bedsheet, repeating the act of writing, except that our words would be nothing more than a decorative tile or a doormat uttering faded words of welcome. Then, finally, in the evening, an evening with no dusk, night abruptly succeeding day, we reached Nova Lisboa, a railway town on the plateau, which is now only a vague memory of provincial cafés and dusty shopwindows, and the restaurant where we had supper, our rifles between our knees, watched by mulattos wearing dark glasses and standing before immemorial beers, and whose frozen features had the smooth consistency of scars; throughout the meal, I felt as if I were part of a preamble to the St. Valentine's Day Massacre, ready for a Prohibition-style shoot-out, and I raised my fork to my mouth with the languid tedium of an Al Capone, practicing cruel smiles in the mirror; even today, you know, when I leave the cinema, I still light my cigarette the way Humphrey Bogart did, until the sight of my own reflection in the glass brings me back down to earth: instead of walking into the arms of Lauren Bacall, I am, in fact, heading for an apartment in some low-class *bairro*, and the illusion falls apart with the heartrending crash of a myth destroyed. I put the key in the door (is it Humphrey Bogart or me?), I hesitate, then go in, look at the engraving in the hallway (it's definitely me now), and slump onto the sofa with the punctured-tire sigh of a Cinderella in reverse. Just as when I leave here, once I've told you this strange story and have, at a camel's pace, drunk the contents of every bottle in sight, I'll find myself outside in the cold, far from your silence and your smile, lonely as an orphan, with my hands in my pockets, watching the sun rise and filled with an anxiety the color and texture of cream, an anxiety only heightened by the macabre pallor of the trees. Besides, the early mornings, grimy, cold, sour, full of bitterness and rancor, are always a torment to me. Nothing is alive then, and an indefinable threat begins to grow and draw near, pursuing me, filling my chest, preventing me from breathing freely; the creases in the pillow turn to stone, the furniture bristles with hostility. The houseplants extend parched tentacles to grab me, on the other side of the mirror left-handed objects reject my proffered fingers, my slippers disappear, my bathrobe has ceased to exist, and inside me, stubborn, insistent, painfully slow, is that train crossing Angola, from Nova Lisboa to Luso, filled to overflowing with uniformed men, their weary heads nodding and banging against the windows as they search for that impossibility, sleep.

Do you know General Machado? No, don't frown, don't rack your brains, no one knows General Machado, one hundred out of every hundred Portuguese have never heard of him, yet the planet continues to turn despite their ignorance of his existence, and personally, I hate him. He was the father of my maternal grandmother, and on Sundays, before lunch, she would point proudly at the photograph of what looked like a rather unpleasant, mustachioed fireman, the owner of numerous medals that thundered at us from the glass cabinet in the living room along with other equally useless trophies of war, but which the family seemed to venerate as if they were relics. For years, you see, I had to listen every week, bored and apathetic, to my grandmother's excited voice recounting episodes from the fireman's worthy life and which, in her eyes, took on epic proportions: for years and years General Machado poisoned my Sunday lunch, injecting the meat with the indigestible mold of his ramrod-straight dignity, whose Victorian rigidity sickened me. And it was that same baleful creature—whose bulging eyes, the eyes of a prefect or a priest, gazed reprovingly down on me from the wall, refusing me even the dubious absolution that usually hovers like a halo in the yellowing smiles of old photos—who built, or oversaw the construction, or planned the construction, or both planned and oversaw the construction of the railway on which we were traveling; our train, with an attachment at the front for detonating mines, rattled across a plain that had neither beginning nor end, as we laboriously chewed our combat ration of canned food with a lack of appetite already imbued with the panic-fear of death, which, over a period of twenty-three months, grew its greenish mushrooms in my damp insides. In the officers' mess in Luso, a town that resembled a kind of Bairro da Madre de Deus of geometric streets and cheap houses set down on the Bunda Plateau, in the same Disneyland spirit that made of the Estado Novo a constant aberration by excess or defect, erring on the side of either sentimentalism or repression, there I saw, for the last time in many months, curtains, wineglasses, white women, and rugs: gradually, the things I had been used to for years and years moved away from me, family, comfort, quiet, even the pleasure of certain harmless annoyances, or the gentle melancholy that is the privilege of those who lack for nothing, or the romantic *ennui* born of an illusory belief in one's own superiority. For example, a postprandial sadness took the place of the newspaper crossword puzzle, when I would entertain myself filling in the little blank squares with irksome lucubrations that veered between the utterly idiotic and the profoundly commonplace, which are, indeed, the natural boundaries of Lusitanian thought, the metaphysical equivalents of the poems that accompany the paper carnations people give to their sweethearts at Carnival time. You see, we belong to a land where vivacity stands in for talent and where dexterity takes the place of creativity, in fact, I often think that we are little more than a bunch of dexterous mental defectives mending the blown fuses of the soul with some temporary wire device. Perhaps my being here with you is just another such device to save me from the low tide of despair threatening me, a despair whose cause I do not know, but which, at night, wraps me in its sticky slime, drowns me in anxiety and fear, traces a mustache of sweat above my upper lip, and makes my knees knock like the chattering dentures of a sleeping porter. No, I mean it, dusk falls and my heart starts to pound, I can feel it in my pulse, there's a tightening in my stomach, my bladder hurts, my ears hum, as if some indefinable thing waiting to burst forth were throbbing inside my chest: one of these days, the porter will find me lying naked on the bathroom floor, toothpaste and blood dribbling from one corner of my mouth, my eyes grown suddenly huge, staring at nothing, my bloodless body already beginning to smell and fill with gases. You'll read about it in the newspaper, you won't believe it, you'll read the item again, check name, profession, age, and, two hours later, you'll have forgotten all about it and you'll come here, as you usually do, to anchor your silence in this small bay of empty glasses, the slightest movement setting your Indian bracelets tinkling, bracelets that recall a mythical London lost in the mists of the past, in the days when Bob Dylan was still talking and the legs of the salesgirls in Selfridges were almost as attractive as the smiles of the policemen.

Another vodka? I know I haven't finished mine yet, but I always get upset at this point in my narrative, I know it was six years ago, but I still get upset: we were traveling in convoy along sandy roads from Luso down to the Land at the End of the World, Lucusse, Luanguinga, past troops guarding the road construction site, past the ugly, uniform desert, villages surrounded by barbed wire, the prefabricated buildings of the barracks, past the cemetery silence of the refectories and the slowly collapsing corrugated iron shacks, heading down to the Land at the End of the World, twelve hundred miles from Luanda, it was late January, it was raining, and we were going to die, we were going to die and it was raining, raining. Sitting in the cabin of a truck beside the driver, cap pulled low over my eyes, an endless cigarette vibrating in my hand, I began my painful apprenticeship in dying.

E

Sago Coutinho, some one hundred ninety miles south of Luso and on the frontier with Zambia, consisted of a nipple of dusty red earth between two desolate plains, a barracks, various villages headed by chiefs whom the Portuguese government obliged to wear ridiculous carnivalesque outfits involving stars and ribbons, a PIDE headquarters, an administration building, Mete Lenha's café, and the leper colony: once a week, in the noisy silence you get in Africa when it suddenly goes quiet, I would ring the chapel bell that hung in the middle of a circle of apparently deserted huts, and dozens of shapeless larvae would begin to emerge, limping, trotting, dragging themselves along, from behind bushes and trees and from huts, out of the vague contours of the shadows, Bosch-like larvae of all ages, on whose backs fluttered a fringe of rags, like feathers, as they advanced toward me like the monstrous toads of a child's nightmare, reaching out with their ulcerated stumps for the bottles of medicine. Senhor Jonatão, the black nurse from the public health delegation, who smiled all the time like the Chinamen in _Tintin_ stories, distributed the pills with all the macabre majesty of a eucharistic ritual for the living dead, some of whom, already blind, would turn, on no one in particular, empty sockets reduced to a damp blue mist of repellent mucus. Children without fingers, tormented by flies, gathered around, dumb with amazement, women with gargoyle features murmured words that their ruined palates turned into an incomprehensible jumble of moans, and I imagined the resurrection of the flesh in the catechism as bits of intestine rising up from the graves in cemeteries, like a slow awakening of snakes. It was almost as if all the pale people in this bar, holding whispered conversations, hunched in fetal positions, putting the boneless tentacles of their arms about each other's necks, were to rush pell-mell not into the tame, complicit night of a Lapa* composed of snoring basset hounds and countesses but into an excessively bright day lit by the vertical sun of operating theatres or boxing rings that pitilessly revealed baggy eyes, wrinkles, crow's feet, sagging breasts, and empty expressions that no amount of Cognac could animate. Regally seated on a rickety chair, Senhor Jonatão absolved with iodine the proffered wounds, painting them with expeditious extreme unctions, useless incantations against the presence of death, and I wandered aimlessly from village to village, startling skeletal old ladies who squatted in the entrances to their huts and whose skirts, too wide for their narrow hips, resembled the paper sleeves on drinking straws. And then there was the smell of putrefaction from the cassava drying on the mats, the coming rain that you could sense in the damp air, dried excrement resembling the cardboard turds you can buy at Carnival, plump rats rummaging among the rubbish, the flat plain in the distance crossed by a river as narrow and sinuous as one of the veins in your hand, and the bats

---

* Lapa is an expensive area of Lisbon and home to many foreign embassies as well as the Portuguese prime minister's official residence.

waiting for evening in what remained of the Temple of Diana that had once been a settler's house, now submerged in grass, the color of oblivion.

Gago Coutinho was also the café owned by Mete Lenha, a white man with such a terrible stutter that, in his efforts to speak, he would contort his face into the grimaces of someone straining over a bowel movement; he was married to a sort of large gas cylinder, adorned with garish necklaces, who was always complaining to the officers about the pinches with which the soldiers paid homage to her enormous buttocks, which were, it must be said, difficult to discern in a woman who resembled a vast ambulant gluteus maximus and whose very face had something anal about it and whose nose was like a painfully swollen hemorrhoid; the café sold innocuous cold drinks on the long, long Sunday afternoons, and it was there, for the first time, that the lieutenant confidingly opened his wallet to show me the photograph of his maid and, leaning back in the wrought-iron chair far too small for his gigantic shoulder blades, presented me with the synthesis of a whole lifetime of thought:

"If you want to keep your domestics happy, stick your ladle in the soup."

In the gloomy civilian hospital, like some dead-and-alive provincial boardinghouse, its walls blistered with patches of damp, the malaria patients shook with fever on the front steps, in the corridor, in the consulting room, in the cubicle set aside for injections, as they waited for their dose of quinine with the immemorial placidity of all Africans, for whom time, distance, and life possess a profundity and a meaning impossible to explain to anyone born among alarm clocks and the tombs of *infantas*, goaded on by the dates of battles and monasteries and by time clocks. Seated at my bunker of a desk, where I installed myself and my textbook knowledge, I watched misery and hunger parade past all morning with the monotonous serenity of September rain, and the only response afforded me by my inadequacy and powerlessness was the handful of vitamins I gave to the soldiers, sweetened with an embarrassed, apologetic smile. Prevented from hunting or fishing, with no fields to work, imprisoned by the barbed wire and the Portuguese administration's handouts of dried fish, spied on by the PIDE, tyrannized by the *cipaios*—the black policemen in the pay of the whites—the tribesmen fled into the jungle, where the MPLA,* the invisible enemy, was hiding, forcing us to wage a crazy ghostly war. With each wound inflicted in an ambush or by a mine, the same question kept troubling me—me, who had been rushed, bemused and bewildered, into that dusty hellhole, me, a child of right-wing youth movements, of Catholic journals and state-controlled newspapers, the nephew of catechists and a close friend of the Holy Family who, safe beneath a glass dome, often used to visit us at home: is it the guerrillas who are murdering us or Lisbon, or is it the Americans, the Russians, the Chinese, or the whole fucking lot of them determined to screw us good and proper in the name of certain interests that escape me now, and who plunged me without warning into this asshole of the world full of red dust and sand, to play checkers with the aged captain promoted from sergeant who smelled like an apathetic, menopausal clerk, tormented by the chronic griping of colitis. Is there anyone who can explain this absurdity to me, the letters I receive that speak to me of a world made foreign and unreal

---

* The MPLA (*Movimento Popular da Libertação de Angola*) fought against Portugal in the war for independence from 1961 to 1975 and against UNITA (*União Nacional para a Independência Total de Angola*) and FNLA (*Frente Nacional de Libertação de Angola*) in the ensuing civil war from 1975 to 2002. It has been the ruling party in Angola since 1975.

by distance, the calendars that I cover in crosses as I count off the days separating me from my return home, finding only an endless tunnel of months stretching out before me, a dark tunnel of months down which I hurl myself, bellowing, a wounded, uncomprehending ox, so incapable of understanding what is going on that he ends up burying his sad, moist snout in the chicken bones and spaghetti in his mess tin, just as here, in your company, I realize that I feel like a horse with my snout in the nosebag of my vodka, munching the sour hay of my lemon slice.

After supper, the officers' Jeeps would drive from hut to hut, headlights blinking like fireflies, looking for quick, cheap love in airless huts lit by the stuttering wicks of oil lamps that gave the mud walls the illusory look of chapels. You would arrive with your tube of antivenereal cream in your pocket and apply it to your cock through your fly, open like a cloth vulva, beneath the indifferent gaze of women whose teeth had been filed into triangles, women who crouched on the bed, faces coldly averted like the women in certain Picasso paintings, and on whose lips flickered disdainful *Guernicas*. Normally, the children slept on that same mattress, along with the chickens and the occasional decrepit ancestor lost in a mummy's mummified nightmares and mumbling dream hieroglyphs. The lieutenant fucked with the peak of his cap turned around to the back and his pistol at his waist, while his aide, rifle in hand, stood guard, the operations officer ordered a sewing machine from Luso and spent the early hours hemming trousers beside a splendid black woman with energetic, pendant breasts like those of the she-wolf of Rome, and the captain, my checkers partner, sat at the wheel of the Jeep and asked prepubescent girls to masturbate him in exchange for tubes of mints: the white man came with a whip, sang the sergeant, accompanying himself on the guitar, the white man came with a whip and beat the chief and his tribe, the white man came with a whip and beat the chief and his tribe.

You'll never know what it's like to wake in the middle of the night, a moonless night, with an urgent need to urinate and have to go outside to take a piss, with absolutely nothing around you, no light, no barracks, no shapes, just the sound of your invisible pee and the frozen stars in the half-orange of the sky, far too distant, far too small, and far too inaccessible, always ready to disappear, because the morning comes suddenly and, before you know it, it's bright daylight, to wake in the middle of the night and feel in the stillness and the silence the numberless sleep of Africa, and there we were, legs splayed, in T-shirt and shorts, tiny, vulnerable, ridiculous, alien, with no past and no future, adrift in the startled narrowness of the present, scratching our thrush-infected balls. You would doubtless have been leaning at this bar, with the same cigarette in your left hand, the same glass in your right, and the same utter indifference in your eyes, inalterable and motionless, a bird with painted eyelids perched on the branch of your stool, making your Indian bracelets tinkle to the precise music of your gestures. I like your gestures, by the way, as automatic and slow as the hands on the clock pursuing their stubborn trajectory. Anyway, I would finish peeing and the bubbles would hiss on the ground as if my bladder were a kettle reaching a boil, and then I'd go back inside, stretch out on my enamel-white bed in the infirmary until the first bugle call jerked me awake from my diffuse, vaporous dreams.

From time to time, this asshole of the world would receive unexpected visitors: officers from the general staff in Luanda, preserved in the formaldehyde of air-conditioning; fifty-something South African women who, in a fit of menopausal heat, would kiss the patients; two cabaret artistes clumsily kicking their fat legs on a tabletop stage, accompanied by an exhausted accordion: they had supper in the mess beside the commanding officer, who was bursting with pride, his shyness wrapped in the smiles of an overage adolescent, while the lieutenant who screwed his own cook prowled around, sniffing the women's décolletages in silent ecstasy. The chaplain contritely lowered virgin eyelids over the breviary of his soup.

"Forty years of accumulated sperm," said the elderly captain, sizing him up from a distance. "If that guy ever came, he'd drown the lot of us in the holy water from his balls."

The actresses ended up spending the night at the PIDE headquarters, watched over by bad-tempered agents with threatening, indecipherable eyebrows. It was said that the inspector's wife, a skinny Spanish woman who looked like a contortionist past her prime and who spoke in loud circus tones, used to torture the prisoners herself, inventing crude martyrdoms like some Lucrezia Borgia of the suburbs. Later on, in Baixa do Cassanje, I heard about a black man, a Jinga, being hanged for the edification of the village, and about other blacks who were ordered to dig a hole in the jungle, climb down into it, and wait patiently to have their heads blown off before being covered in sand, like having an earth blanket pulled over the blood of their corpses.

"Bastards, bastards, bastards," said the lieutenant, stunned.

The white man came with a whip, sang the sergeant, accompanying himself on the guitar, and beat the chief and his tribe.

F

Have you ever noticed how at this hour of the night and with this amount of alcohol in your blood, the body begins to emancipate itself from you, refusing to light your cigarette, grasping your glass with a certain tactile clumsiness, wandering about inside your clothes with a gelatinous fluidity? From two o'clock in the morning onward, the charm of bars, don't you think, consists precisely in the fact that it isn't your soul liberating itself from its earthly envelope and rising straight up to heaven with a mystical fluttering of white drapery, the way the dead are shown in prayer-book images, but your somewhat startled flesh freeing itself from the spirit and commencing the glutinous dance of a slowly melting wax figure that ends in tears of remorse at dawn, when the first oblique light of day reveals to us, with radioscopic implacability, the sad skeleton of our hopeless solitude. If we take a good look at ourselves, we can already begin to see the shape of our bones, which the commas formed by the dark circles under our eyes and the circumflex of our mouth disguise with melancholy smiles from which dangle, like the injured, inert arm of an accident victim, a few withered remnants of irony. The guy at the next table, who, after his tenth glass of muscatel, is now leaning seventeen degrees to port, as rigid as a tottering, velvet-jacketed Tower of Pisa on the verge of catastrophic collapse, could easily be Amedeo Modigliani searching in the bottom of his glass for the murdered face of a woman, Fernando Pessoa[*] might well inhabit that bespectacled gentleman sitting over there by the mirror, and in his pear brandy there perhaps pulsates the thrilling helm he mentions in his *Maritime Ode*, or perhaps my brother Scott Fitzgerald, whom Blondin[†] compared to an Irish rugby three-quarter-back, will, at any moment, sit down at our table and explain to us the desperate tenderness of the night and the impossibility of love, well, you know how it is, vodka blurs time and cancels distance, your name is really Ava Gardner and you consume eight bullfighters and six crates of Logan's whisky a week, and, as for me, my real name is Malcolm Lowry, as dark as the grave wherein my friend is laid, I write immortal novels, I say *¿Le gusta este jardín, que es suyo? Evite que sus hijos lo destruyan,*[‡] and on the final page, my corpse, like that of a dead dog, will be thrown down a ravine. We have all come here today to occupy the innocent, imitation Carlos Botelho[§]–pink Lapa of this, the low tide of our silent drinking sprees, on the surface of which flickers, now and then and By Appointment to Her Majesty the Queen, the flame of genius, and above our anointed heads hover the tongues of fire of

---

[*] Fernando Pessoa (1888–1935), probably Portugal's finest poet, wrote under various pseudonyms with distinct biographies, temperaments, philosophies, and writing styles. *Maritime Ode* is a long poem written under one of these pseudonyms, Álvaro de Campos.

[†] Antoine Blondin (1922–1991) was a French novelist and sportswriter.

[‡] "Do you like this garden of yours? Then don't let your children destroy it."

[§] Carlos Botelho (1899–1982) was a painter and illustrator famed for the pastel shades of his many paintings of Lisbon.

Johnnie Holy Spirit Walker: Utrillo, who crumpled up picture post-cards as he painted, Soutine, he of the choirboys and the tortured houses, Gomes Leal wearing the innocent, thunderous poverty of an elderly child, and the two of us watching in amazement this procession of sublime clowns accompanied by circus music. It might seem strange to you, but I used to live surrounded by ghosts in an old house that was like a ghost of itself, from the large front door flanked by stone pineapples to the trunk of bones for anatomy classes, kept safely wrapped in a sweet perfume of incense and gangrene until it was my turn to study them. Stray cats used to hide in the branches of the fig tree in the garden like furtive fruits, their eyes dripping the green milk of instant distrust, the glass window of the wood-burning stove reflected the opalescent clarity of Cesário's poetry, and in the living room, the portrait of Antero de Quental,[*] his painful beauty seared by genius, put the modest mustaches of my grandfathers to shame with the disorderly ocean of his blond beard, on which lay shipwrecked the broken debris of tercets. My father, as thin and angular as a Mormon, sat adrift on his armchair, propelled by the ship's funnel of his pipe. Shadows filled the geometric volumes of the neighboring buildings, designed by a sad Soulages. And I masturbated in my bedroom beneath the color photograph of the Benfica team, in the hope that I would one day become the literary equivalent of José Águas, who, crouched in the middle, defied the world with the marmoreal pride of a triumphant discus-thrower.

In that asshole of the world, disguised in my camouflage uni-

---

[*] Antero de Quental (1842–1891), a Portuguese poet and political agitator, was the guiding light of the reformist, modernizing group of writers and thinkers known as the Generation of 1870.

form that gave me the equivocal appearance of a disillusioned chameleon, I postponed my departure to Stockholm, on board a boat made of printed paper, in order to travel by helicopter, with plasma bags between my knees, to pluck from the jungle those wounded in ambushes who were hoisted up to us like shipwreck victims by their stupefied but unscathed comrades. The army nurse, who felt sick at the sight of blood, stood at the door of the improvised operating theatre, bent double like a penknife, vomiting onto a bench the bean stew he'd eaten for lunch, and I, rigid with rage, imagined how pleased my family would be if they could see, all of them together and wearing broad-brimmed hats like in Rembrandt's *Anatomy Lesson*, the competent, responsible doctor they had always wanted me to be, patching up with needle and thread the heroic defenders of the empire, who paraded their incomprehension and horror along jungle paths: *C'est un peu, dans chacun de ces hommes, Mozart assassiné,* I repeated furiously to myself, as I debrided tibias, rotated tourniquets, regulated the flow from the oxygen bottle, and prepared the amputees to travel on to Luso, as soon as day broke, in a light aircraft provided by the Portuguese Air Force, while, in the room next door, the stretcher-bearers searched for donors' veins and the lieutenant restlessly watched my every gesture with growing anxiety. During that time of ashes, while I worked on the peeled stump of a limb or stuffed protruding intestines back into a stomach, words have never seemed so superfluous, bereft of the sense I had always previously given them, stripped of weight, timbre, meaning, color, never had anger risen up in me so pointlessly, never had political

---

* "Each of these men is, in a small way, Mozart murdered." From *Terre des Hommes* by Antoine de Saint-Exupéry.

exile in Paris seemed so stupid: if someone asks me why I'm still in the army, I tell them that the revolution is made from within, that's what the captain with the wire-rimmed glasses and the membranous fingers would say from behind his eternal cigarette; that same captain once drew his pistol on a scrawny PIDE agent for kicking a young, heavily pregnant woman and then drummed him out of the company, ignoring the man's bitter threats, the same captain whose trunks were full of books and foreign magazines that told me things I didn't know, the same captain I joined months later on the barbed-wire island of Ninda, by the river, for the compassless crossing of one long night.

The Africans' tribal drumbeats were concertos of panicking, tachycardiac hearts, only restrained by the darkness from galloping wildly off in the direction of their own anxiety, just as, for example, my trembling legs move closer to yours beneath our accomplice, the tabletop. The eyes of the drummers looked like phosphorescent boiled eggs, with no pupils, lit by the grass bonfires intended to stretch the skins for the drums or by the buttocks that swayed, suspended in the void, like the lights of a train moving off. Each hut, flanked by an identical miniature hut dedicated to the god Zumbi, the lord of ancestors and the dead, took on the formless shape of disquiet and terror, where the mongrel dogs added their frightened barking to the crying of children and the interrogative clucking of hens, imperfect birds fated to end their days on the barbecue. The darkness was full of galleries, corridors, and steps that these sounds penetrated as if desperately searching, leafing through shadows, sifting faces, rummaging in the empty drawers of silence, looking for their own echoes, just as sometimes, to our terror and surprise, we find a cruel reminder of the person we once were in long-forgotten objects stored away on the shelves of cupboards. The sweat of their bodies, thick and juicy, had a completely different texture from the sad, shivering drops running down my spine, and, faced by a people whose inexhaustible vitality I'd glimpsed years before in Louis Armstrong's sunny trumpet-playing, guaranteed to drive out neurasthenia and bitterness with the sheer muscular joy of his song, I felt like the melancholy heir to an old country, moribund and ungainly, to a Europe replete with palaces like carbuncles and ailing cathedrals like bladder stones. At that hour, in my city castrated by the police and by censorship, people would be coagulating with cold at bus stops, blowing clouds of steam from their mouths, like the bubbles of a comic strip banned by the government. Bare-chested, my father would stand in front of the bathroom mirror shaving with his usual quick, precise movements, inside my mother's womb a child ready to be born would be kicking blindly at the fleshly bars of his prison, and in the great black bed that had always symbolized home, my mother would be reaching out one sleepy arm for the breakfast tray. It occurred to me that, whether out of shyness or embarrassment, I had never felt able to show them how much I loved them, and that long-repressed tenderness filled my mouth with the bitter taste of remorse and the pain of having frustrated their small hopes by transforming my life into a random series of disastrous somersaults. Grandiose plans, in which Freud, Goethe, and St. Francis of Assisi converged and combined, began to germinate inside my repentant brain, like beans on the damp cotton batting of school experiments, pocket miracles for mongoloid Lavoisiers: I swore to myself with the fervor of a pilgrim setting out on the road to Santiago that, if I returned home in one piece, I would not rest until I had fashioned out of my confused state of nothingness the bronze image of the ideal husband and son, based on the pictures in the death announcements stuck between the pages of my grandmother's missal, creatures replete with qualities and virtues *à la* St. Thérèse of Lisieux and of whom I knew only their resigned smiles. I might even join the Scouts and, complete with whistle, shorts, and an air of patient authority, shepherd a group of spotty adolescents past the horse-drawn carriages in the Museu dos Coches or wander the streets on the lookout for old people with walking sticks having difficulty crossing the road. I would join the Brotherhood of the Holy Cross, become a clarinetist in the local band, a collector of false teeth, all in order to expel from the unbearably quiet evenings my eternal, deleterious desire to escape. I would silence forever the little voice in my head stubbornly demanding feats worthy of Zorro. And at the end of a painful illness borne with Christian resignation and consoled by the sacraments of Our Holy Mother Church, I would take my place in the pantheon of my grandmother's missal, joining that extensive gallery of kindly bores, and be offered up as an example to my indifferent grandchildren, who would view my absurdly tepid existence with rage.

G

*N*inda. Ninda's eucalyptus trees in the vast nights of Eastern Angola, seething with insects and the sound of grinding, saliva-less jaws made by the dry leaves above, as dry as our tense mouths in the dark: the attack began over by the landing strip, on the far side of the village, where moving lights flickered on and off like Morse code. The huge moon shed its oblique light on the prefab barracks, on the sentry posts protected by sandbags and wooden logs, and on the zinc rectangle of the powder magazine. Naked and barely awake, I stood at the door of the first-aid hut and watched as soldiers wielding guns raced over to the barbed wire, and then came the voices, the shouts, the spurts of red that emerged from the rifles, and all of that, plus the tension, the lack of decent food, the ramshackle accommodation, the water transformed by filters into a pap of indigestible cartridge paper, and the gigantic, unbelievable absurdity of the war, made me feel that I was living in a strange, unreal, fluctuating atmosphere, one that I encountered again later in psychiatric hospitals, islands of despair and misery from which Lisbon defended itself with walls and iron bars, just as bodily tissue protects itself from foreign bodies by wrapping them in fibrous capsules. Confined in dilapidated wards, wearing the uniform of the ill, we walked our incommunicable dreams, our formless angst, around the sandy parade ground of the barracks, viewing our past through the inverted binoculars of letters from home and photos kept at the bottoms of suitcases beneath the bed, prehistoric remains from which we could reconstruct, like biologists examining a single bone, the monstrous skeleton of our grief.

It occurred to me that when news of the ceasefire came on the radio, we would all have to undergo a painful re-apprenticeship in life, like those hemiplegics who exercise the recalcitrant spaghetti of their limbs on gym contraptions and in swimming pools, and that we might remain forever incapable of walking, reduced to the wheelchair of paralytic resignation, observing the simplicity of the everyday just as Charlie Chaplin in *Modern Times* views the terrifying machines implacably grinding him down: escaping the porter and the phony indulgence of doctors, like sheets of cardboard painted with smiley faces, and discovering gradually, farther down the hill, the geometric morning of the city chopped up into faded lozenges of glazed tiles, entering a phantasmagorical café for your first coffee as a free man, seeing the retirees playing dominoes in the eternal pose of Cézanne's cardplayers, and feeling that you have ceased forever to belong to that clear, direct world where things have the consistency of things, with no subterfuges, no hidden meanings, and that the days can still offer us, despite sore throats, bill collectors, and car payments, the surprise of the winning lottery ticket of an unsolicited smile. You, for example, with your aseptic, competent, dandruff-free air of an executive secretary, would you be able to breathe inside a painting by Bosch, overwhelmed by demons, lizards, gnomes hatching from eggshells, and staring gelatinous eyeballs? Lying in a hollow, waiting for the attack to end, watching the stiff, top-hatted silhouettes of the eucalyptus trees like glum seconds in a duel, with my G3 rifle useless in my sweating hands and a cigarette stuck in my mouth like a toothpick in a croquette, I discovered myself to be a Beckett character waiting for the mortar grenade of a redemptive Godot. The novels as yet unwritten accumulated in the attic of my mind like ancient bits of apparatus reduced to a pile of disparate parts that I would never manage to put together again, the women with whom I would never sleep would offer to others their splayed thighs like frogs in a biology class, and I would not be there to cut them open with the eager penknife of my tongue, my unborn child would remain forever the unlikely fruit of a far-off afternoon in Tomar, in a room in the officers' mess with the window wide open to the parade ground, with the sunlight sieving through the acacia leaves and us celebrating in bed the ardent liturgy of an all-too-fleeting desire. Tomar: a mattress that creaked like the sole of a shoe, urgent embraces, my erect penis, damp with thirst, thick with veins, flowering red, in Pessanha's* words, her hand rubbing it against her breasts, her mouth drinking it, her heels digging into my buttocks, the exhausted silence afterward of marionettes deserted by the fingers that worked them. Now, when I meet her, it's as if I were looking at the pale rectangle left behind by a picture frame that contained a painting we no longer remember, and I struggle in vain to make out, behind those features grown old and serious, trying so hard to adopt an expression of benign camaraderie that was never hers, the young, happy face that I loved, closing around her own pleasure like the petals of a flower. And yet that is how she remains for me, despite the wear and tear of the years and the bitterness of failed reconcili-

---

* Camilo Pessanha (1867–1926) was a Portuguese symbolist poet.

ations, the wounds of mutual lies and the disillusion of our final parting: the dark, slender girl with large serious eyes, whom I met on the beach, where she was watching the waves with all the lofty majesty of a bored carnivore who had suddenly withdrawn into some painful, motionless meditation, shooing us off into the shadowy corner occupied by forgotten, futile objects. Do you remember Paul Simon's song "Fifty Ways to Leave Your Lover?"

Ninda: the maize outside the barbed-wire fence spent all night leafing through its dry pages, the witch doctor sucked with brutal voracity at the necks of decapitated chickens. The captain and I played chess at the table in the dining room, among the crumbs and the peelings, advancing an interrogative, reticent pawn rather like a finger fearfully probing an infected boil, or we would sit outside talking, on chairs made from the curved staves of barrels, estimating our approximate positions in the darkness from the echo that came back to us of our own voices, like distressed bats looking for each other. Into my untidy inner wax museum of doctors and poets, where Vesalius* and Bocage† discussed picaresque, clandestine anatomical details beneath the chaste, reproving gaze of General Fernandes Costa, he of the sonnets in the *Almanaque Bertrand*, from whom, as a child, I shamelessly plagiarized lines that had all the glassy glitter of the cheap metaphors I loved, an impetuous crowd of illustrious bearded men rushed in, singing first "The Internationale" and then "La Marseillaise," boldly replacing Dr. Júlio Dantas, Dr. Augusto de Castro, and another

---

* Andreas Vesalius (1514–1564) is often referred to as the founder of modern human anatomy.

† Manuel Maria Barbosa du Bocage (1765–1805) was a Portuguese poet of French parentage. Salazar placed his scurrilous and erotic verse on the list of banned books.

dozen or so thick-skinned individuals sitting on Empire sofas whispering historical dramas embroidered in the cross-stitch of empty small talk. The captain introduced me in passing to Marx, who regarded me from afar and mumbled unintelligibly into his collar about economics, to Lenin in a toupee conspiring with a group of ardent frock coats, to Rosa Luxemburg limping sadly through the streets of Berlin, to Jean Jaurès shot dead in a restaurant, napkin around his neck, reminding me of murdered Chicago gangsters spinning round and round in barbers' chairs, accompanied by the sound of shattering mirrors and bottles, and I imagined going into the house with them to watch my terrified relatives fleeing to the safety of their class icons, brandishing the exorcisory garlic of an image of Sãozinha at the scornful Socialist vampires threatening them, oh horrors, with nationalizing the family china. The squad who went out at night to guard the barracks, crouching in the low, yellowish, anemic scrub that grew in the sand, would return in the dark, pass beneath the light surrounded by a lampshade of insects, and disperse silently to their respective huts, where depth of sleep was measured by the intensity of the odor given off by the bodies that lay in random piles like the dead in the mass graves of Auschwitz, and I asked the captain, What have they done to my people, what have they done to us, sitting here waiting in this landlocked place, imprisoned by three rows of barbed wire in a land that doesn't belong to us, dying of malaria and bullets, whose whistling trajectory sounds like a nylon thread vibrating, fed by unreliable supply lines whose arrival or not is dependent on frequent accidents en route, on ambushes and land mines, fighting an invisible enemy, fighting the endless days that never pass, fighting homesickness, indignation, and remorse, fighting the dark nights as thick and opaque as a mourning veil that I draw over my head in order to sleep, just as, when I was a child, I used the edge of the sheet to protect myself from the phosphorous-blue eyes of my ghosts.

Tell me something: how do you sleep? Face down, thumb in mouth, in a state of abandon vaguely reminiscent of a lost childhood fragility, or do you sleep wearing earplugs and a black mask like those decadent Hollywood movie stars or femmes fatales driven to despair by loneliness and champagne, by nightmares peopled with divorces, plastic surgeons, and yelping wirehaired terriers like caricatures of Audrey Hepburn? I bet you read esoteric poets before you turn out the light, men with complicated mustaches who sometimes haunt this bar, hoping to hide their unmitigated mediocrity behind a gin fizz, and who are admired by flat-chested girls and who smoke crumpled Gauloise cigarettes as greedily as unkempt old ladies in nursing homes devour their Sunday slice of sponge cake. I bet you have an engraving by Vieira da Silva* on your bedroom wall and, on your bedside table, a photo of the talentless movie director with whom you have a somewhat disenchanted relationship, I bet you wake in the morning as torpid as a chrysalis hovering eternally between larva and butterfly, then stumble blindly into the kitchen in the unrealistic hope that your first cup of coffee, gulped down among the dirty pots and pans, will guarantee that your horoscope wasn't telling lies when it promised you that efficient, waistcoated, wise, and gentle research executive with graying temples and designer tie, in charge of some multinational soap manufacturer. For my part, well, I don't expect very much from life: my daughters are growing up in a house that con-

---

*Maria Helena Vieira da Silva (1908–1992), French-Portuguese abstractionist artist.

tains fewer and fewer memories of me, full of furniture drowned in the dark waters of the past, and then there are the women I meet only to abandon or to be abandoned by with a feeling of quiet mutual disappointment in which there is not even room for the kind of resentment that is like a retrospective sign of a sort of love, and I grow old gracelessly in an apartment that's far too large for me, sitting at an empty desk, watching the night and the glittering river through the closed balcony windows that reflect back at me a man sitting utterly still, chin in his hands, whom I refuse to recognize, but who continues to stare at me with stubborn resignation. Perhaps the war has helped to make me the person I am today whom I deep down reject: a melancholic bachelor whom no one phones and from whom no one expects a call, who coughs occasionally just to feel as if he had company, and whom the cleaning lady will find one day sitting in his rocking chair in his undershirt, mouth agape, his purple fingers trailing on the November-colored hair of the carpet.

H

———

*L*isten. Look at me and listen, I so need you to listen, to listen with the same anxious attention with which we used to listen to the calls on the radio from the company under fire, the voice from the communications officer calling, begging, in the helpless tones of a shipwreck victim, forgetting all about the security code he should have been using, and the captain climbing into the Mercedes truck with half a dozen volunteers and driving out past the barbed wire, skidding in the sand, as they set off to find the ambush, listen to me the way I did when I leaned over the mouth of our first casualty in the desperate hope that he was still breathing, the corpse I wrapped in a blanket and left in my room, it was after lunch and my legs felt like cotton batting, I closed the door of the hut and said, Enjoy your nap, the soldiers outside looked at me, but said nothing, No miracles this time, my dears, I thought, staring back at them, He's just having a nap, I explained, and I don't want you to wake him up because he prefers not to be disturbed, and then off I went to treat the wounded lying on sheets of canvas, writhing in pain, the eucalyptuses of Ninda had never seemed so large to me as they did that afternoon, big, black, tall, vertical, frightening, the medic helping me kept saying, Fuck fuck fuck with a northern accent, because we came from all over our gagged country to die in Ninda, from all over our sad country of stone and sea to die in Ninda, Fuck fuck fuck, I repeated along with him in my educated Lisbon accent, the captain got out of the Mercedes looking completely exhausted, his rifle over his shoulder as if it were a useless fishing rod, the people in the village down below peered anxiously up at us, yes, listen to me as I listened to the rapid, anxious beating of blood in my temples, my blood still intact in my temples, through the gaps in the verandah I could see the captain pacing back and forth, clutching to his chest the viaticum of a glass of whisky, talking to himself, all of us talking to ourselves because no one could talk to anyone else, my blood in the captain's glass, take this and drink, O National Union Party, the body of the dead man grew in the room until it burst out of the walls, spread across the sand, and reached the jungle in search of the shot that killed him, the helicopter transported him to Gago Coutinho like someone sweeping some embarrassing garbage under the carpet, more people are killed on the roads in Portugal than in the war in Africa, there have been very few casualties really, 'bye for now, the medic put the surgical instruments in the chrome-plated box, medical penknives, forceps, needle holders, probes, then sat down beside me on the steps of the first-aid post, a kind of miniature vacation home for melancholic retirees, aged butlers, and virginal governesses, and the eucalyptus trees of Ninda kept growing and growing, you and I are sitting here just like he and I did then, April 1971, more than six thousand miles from my city, from my pregnant wife, from my blue-eyed brothers whose affectionate letters curled in fond spirals around my intestines. Fuck, said the medic, who was cleaning his boots with his fingers, Too right, I said, and I don't think I've had such a long conversation with anyone since.

Listen: before that, there was Ferreira's leg, or, rather, the absence of Ferreira's leg, Ferreira having been transformed by an antipersonnel mine into a dying bag of flesh, the tattered thighs of Corporal Mazunguidi, from which I even extracted the metal eyelets of his boots, the cool poultice of morning on my perplexed brow, me reaching the porch of the first-aid post with my shirt stained with blood and receiving like a slap in the face the bright indifference of the day. If the revolution is over, and in a sense it is, it's because the dead of Africa, their mouths full of earth, cannot protest, and hour by hour the people on the right are killing them again, and we, the survivors, are still so doubtful of our own existence that, given our inability to move, we fear that our gestures lack flesh and our words sound, that we are as dead as they are, placed in the lead coffins, blessed by the chaplain, that gave off, despite being welded shut, a strong smell of dung, one for Corporal Pereira, one for Carpinteiro, one for Macaco, who was murdered by a mine just fifty yards from me, the sandbag smashed his ribs against the wheel of his overturned car, I tried to perform heart massage, but his chest was soft and boneless and it crunched beneath my hands, like a sort of pulp, an explosion was all it took to turn Macaco into a rag-and-sawdust puppet, the captain disappeared again into the mess hut and returned with more whisky in his glass, the plain began to drain of color, announcing the coming of night, the medic, still saying Fuck fuck fuck, came and crouched next to us, under our breath we were all saying Fuck, the captain was whispering Fuck into his glass of whisky, the duty officer standing to attention before the flag, his fingers adjusting his beret, was screaming Fuck, the moist, imploring eyes of the stray dogs sniffing at our ankles were moaning Fuck, their eyes as supplicating as those of the people in this bar tonight, moist with resignation and a stupid kind of tenderness, eyes adrift above their glasses of Cognac, eyes accusing their own dead faces, as empty and cloudless as a Magritte sky, dozens of wax figures whose faces occasionally take on the elongated features of china horses, men and women in whose malign, defensive disillusion I refuse to recognize the fragmented image of my own defeat, afraid of belonging to that thicket of burning brambles in which a passionately slow melancholy is being consumed by small, wounded flames, then night fell as suddenly as the curtain at a theatre, covering in absent folds the exhausted actors, the generator kicked in, making a noise like a taxi, the lamp in the mess hut grew dim and then bright, grew dim and then bright, grew dim and then bright, I sat down opposite the captain, at the table that Bichezas had set with the lightning dexterity of a magician, the second lieutenants ate in silence, chins in their plates, just like naughty schoolboys, each one munching away on his own, separated by miles of irrecoverable distance, each night we formed our own anti–Last Supper, our common desire being not to die, you see, that was the one bond uniting us, I don't want to die, you don't want to die, he doesn't want to die, we don't want to die, they don't want to die, the first sergeant, thin, grizzled, obsequious, quizzical, appeared at the door, frozen in an endless salute, clasping in his free hand a bundle of papers for signature, until the captain caught sight of him, looked up, said, Oh dear God, and the fellow vanished, terrified, still clutching his precious file of papers, the captain put down his knife and fork, crossed, on his plate and said, This whole business just gets more and more absurd, and I thought, The ceremony is over, that was the priest's *Ite, missa est, Deo Gratias* and give me your blessing because I'm off, like the guerrillas, past the barbed wire and into the jungle with a piece of cassava in my pocket, a piece of cassava that smells of Carpinteiro's putrefying coffin, I got up in order to see the pumice stone of the moon above the plain and it made me think of Yuri Gagarin's smile when he returned, When I return what kind of smile will mine be? I asked out loud, the second lieutenants turned to look at me, surprised, and the captain reached for the whisky bottle, just as, in the morning, heavy with sleep, one reaches out to the bedside table to quench the horrible jet of noise coming from the alarm clock, to silence its painfully strident bell, drilling into our ears with the imperious blade of a metallic shout.

Listen: in 1962, I was running away from the police at the University Stadium in Lisbon, disorderly crowds of students scattering and making for the canteen, my brother João came home looking very serious and said, Apparently a guy's been killed, the riot police advanced, helmets lowered, in a fury of batons and rifle butts, cars belonging to the PIDE carouseled around the various faculties, on television Salazar wagged his finger, the only thing, by the way, that he ever wagged, bald paunches applauded him with pious fervor, unfortunately, General Delgado was too old to play Nuno Álvares,* and Dom João I, the Mestre de Avis,† was just a little pile of dust in Batalha, so now you have to choose between Paris and the war, because the Castrato, Salazar, is immortal, indeed, the second of Fátima's secrets is a guarantee of the Castrato's immortality, on the voyage out, the ship's band played ancient musty tangos fit for silver wedding anniversaries, I embarked on January 6 and just before that, on New Year's Eve, I locked myself in the bathroom and wept, a piece of Christmas cake lodged in my throat, I washed it down with champagne and when it dropped into my stom-

* Nuno Álvares Pereira (1360–1431) was a highly successful Portuguese general who played a significant role in securing Portugal's independence from Castile. He later became a mystic, was beatified in 1918, and was canonized in 2009.

† Dom João I (1358–1433) ruled Portugal from 1835 until his death. In 1364 he was made grand master of the Order of Aviz, hence "Mestre de Avis."

ach, it made the same sound as the pebbles we used to throw into our grandfather's garden pond, *plof,* creating concentric circles in the lake of our chicken soup at supper, the pond beneath the trees next to the wall by the road where we used to go and smoke a sneaky cigarette, the caretaker took off his hat and explained respectfully, scratching his head, What we need is someone to come and look after us, don't you think, sir? Now if someone came to look after us, after you and me, what do you think he would do first, take me to your house, take you to my house, brush our teeth, put us to bed and talk to us softly until we fell asleep, speak to us of serenity and joy until we fell asleep, speak to us of May 1, 1974, against which the politicians were already inveighing with the empty puff pastry of their vehement speeches, but there was already a growing, irresistible ferment of hope, Caetano's ministers were shitting their pants with fear in Madeira, the PIDE were shitting themselves with fear in Caxias, a festival of red flames spread triumphantly through Lisbon, *quiero que me perdonen los muertos de mi felicidad, los muertos de mi felicidad** in the cold season in Angola, six months of mist and yellow grass burning in the distance, may the dead forgive me when I take your hand, when my knees press against yours, when my mouth is about to touch yours and our eyes close slowly like the petals of a flower at dusk, all my yesterdays are there in that kiss, perhaps the mummies in this bar, in a concerto of breaking hinges, will crumble and fade like vampires at the approach of day, all my yesterdays, you see, What we need, sir, says the caretaker confidently, is for someone to come and look after us, Fuck, said the medic, his chin resting on his knees as he cleaned his boots with his finger, beneath its blanket, the body of our first casualty was beginning to swell up, in fact

---

* "I hope those who died for my happiness will forgive me." From "Pequeña Serenata Diurna," by Cuban singer-songwriter Silvio Rodríguez.

the whole quay is a kind of stone nostalgia, Maria José, and that's when we began to go off the rails, three bottles of whisky a month per officer so that we could keep alight the votive lamp of our stubborn mechanical hearts, the sergeant walked past me and made his nineteenth salute in half an hour, Good evening, Doctor, then disappeared into the darkness to return to his chaos of paperwork, sitting in my barrel-stave chair, I remembered the soldier taking a nap in his lead coffin and the machine gunner calling the fucking bastards who sent us here fucking bastards, those prissy, neatly combed, idiot academics, Fucking bastards, fucking bastards, fucking bastards, the director of the Military Hospital in Tomar summoned me to say, You're being posted to Angola, it was August and the morning sun boiled greenly on the windows, the city afloat on light, the island in the river reflected in the water, posted to Angola with the artillery battalion, Dad, I've been posted to Angola with the artillery battalion, I said in the tiny thread of a voice in which I used to tell him I'd failed an exam at university, the captain came and sat on the other barrel chair and the ice cubes clinked in the dark like coins in a pocket, He was dead on arrival, I told him, and no medical sleight of hand could save him, it really shook me seeing his fair hair, he looked just like me when I was twenty, They were ambushed two yards from the road, said the captain, their blood was all over the bushes, there were traces of blood left where the wounded had been dragged away, the pumice-stone moon got caught in the eucalyptus trees, entangled in the branches, the captain stood up, he looked like Edward G. Robinson in a Fritz Lang film, and he began walking bowlegged over to the quartermaster's store, I asked, Where are you going? the receding shape replied, To hang my balls up in the depot, Doctor, you can give me yours too if you like, because we obviously won't be needing the little fellows for as long as we stay here.

I

—————

*W*hy the hell doesn't anyone talk about this? I'm beginning
to think that the one million five hundred thousand men who went
to Africa never existed and that I'm just giving you some spiel, the
ludicrous plot of a novel, a story I invented to touch your heart—
one-third bullshit, one-third booze, one-third genuine tenderness,
you know the kind of thing—just so that we can cut to the chase
more quickly and end up watching the dawn together in the pale
blue light that seeps in through the shutters and rises up from the
sheets, revealing the sleeping curve of a buttock, the profile of
someone facedown on the mattress, our bodies fused in an entirely
unenigmatic torpor. How long has it been since I slept? I enter the
night like a furtive tramp slipping into a first-class railway car with
a second-class ticket, a clandestine passenger aboard my own
despondency, shrunk into a deathlike inertia that the vodka fires up
with an entirely fake and fickle enthusiasm, and three o'clock in the
morning finds me docking in any bar that's still open, sailing the
stagnant waters of one who has given up all hope of being surprised
by any kind of miracle and is having some difficulty balancing on
his lips the pretend weight of a smile.

How long has it been since I slept? If I close my eyes, a murmurous constellation of pigeons takes flight from the rooftops of my closed eyelids, red with conjunctivitis and tiredness, and their flapping wings send hepatic tremors down my arms; my legs, capable only of a hesitant chicken strut, get tangled in the sheets, damp with fever; inside my head, a slow October rain is falling on the sad geraniums of the past. Each morning, in the mirror, I find I've grown older: my shaving foam transforms me into a pajama-clad Santa Claus whose disheveled hair modestly conceals the perplexed lines on my forehead, and when I brush my teeth, I feel as if I were brushing the mandibles of some museum beast whose ill-fitting dentures wobble about in dusty gums. Sometimes, though, on certain Saturdays, when the oblique sun fills the room with vague, cheering promises, I can still find in my smile a suspicion of my childhood self, and as I soap my armpits, I imagine that wings will sprout from the moss of my underarm hair and I will soar out through the window as lightly as a boat setting sail for the Indies of my local café.

Like on the afternoon of June 22, 1971, in Chiúme, when they called me to the radio to announce to me from Gago Coutinho, letter by letter, the birth of my daughter, golf, india, romeo, lima, the walls lined with photographs of naked women ready for the afternoon's masturbation session, huge tits that began suddenly to recede and advance, and I grabbed the back of the radio officer's chair and thought, Fuck, I'm going to faint.

Chiúme was the farthest-flung of Eastern Angola's hellholes, the farthest from the battalion headquarters, and the most isolated and miserable: the soldiers slept in conical tents in the sand, sharing with the rats the disgusting half-light that seeped through the canvas as if through the skin of a rotting fruit, the sergeants all piled into the ruined house of what had been a trading post, when, before the war, crocodile hunters used to pass through there on their way to the river, and I shared with the captain a room in the command headquarters, where the bats flew in through the holes in the roof, whirling above our beds, flying in stumbling spirals like torn umbrellas in the wind. The sixty or so people confined to the native compound ate the leftover barracks food from rusty tin cans, the women sat crouched in the dust and offered the soldiers the kind of vacant smiles you see on decorated china mugs, except that their toothless mouths lent those smiles an unexpected profundity, and the village chief, a septuagenarian in rags reigning over a people hollow with hunger, reminded me of an old friend of my mother's, an aristocratic woman who lived with her dogs and her daughters in a completely bare apartment in which the deserted walls bore only the rectangular marks where paintings had once been and where the lack of crockery was indicated by a complete absence of dust on the cupboard shelves. A crowd of impatient creditors, baker, milkman, grocer, butcher, etc., swarmed around her threateningly, brandishing unpaid bills, servants loudly demanded their back pay, former fairground wrestlers in overalls, their bodies eroded by the tidal wash of years of cane liquor, were heaving down the stairs, on the way to the pawnshop, the grand piano that occasionally emitted a discordant squeak of protest. Majestically indifferent to the creditors, the maids, the mournful departure of the piano, the dogs peeing on the carpet with a medieval lack of ceremony, my mother's friend sat on a sofa—the springs of which protruded through the velvet like bony clavicles beneath the worn hides of ancient mules—in the proud pose of an exiled princess for whom the clocks go backward, marking only the hours that have been and gone.

The village chief, too, lived in the past, a past of many wives and much land, in an age when his people, from Ninda to Cuando, created the cassava plantations that the DC-3s were now burning down in an attempt to obstruct the progress of the guerrillas advancing from Zambia to the Huambo plateau with the aim of gradually surrounding the cities of the south: I had given him a somewhat rickety armchair taken from the infirmary, and in the late evening sun its white enamel design glittered like the diamonds on a throne, and he sat on this chair, ignoring the hawks swooping in greedy ellipses over his chickens and allowing his distracted gaze to wander at random over the plain as if it were St. Helena, a gaze turned to stone by the memory of sumptuous, long-vanished glories. The war had reduced him to the unusual office of barracks seamstress, just as in Ohnet's novels* Russian counts were obliged to become taxi drivers, and he would spend the afternoons, outside his hut, with an ancient sewing machine that resembled a Mississippi paddle wheeler, on which he would repair the torn trousers of soldiers, making the theatrical gestures of an illusionist rather uncertain of his gifts, just as, I imagine, my hand, insistently stroking your motionless hand, will achieve only a brief night bereft of passion.

I'm fascinated by other people's work, which always puts me in the comfortable position of a spectator freed of all responsibility. When I was a boy, I used to spend hours, enraptured, in the workshop of a cobbler who lived nearby, a tiny room in which there hovered the cool shade of a garden, which was frequented by El Greco–style blind men who sat, striped cane between their knees, talking to the blurred shape hammering away at soles in the background, behind a wall of boots, and who gave off the insecticide

---

*Georges Ohnet (1848–1918) was a popular French novelist fiercely opposed to the realist novels of his day.

smell of polish. The barbers in drugstores, performing ballets of fleeting gestures behind the meek heads of their customers, had me pressing my nose to the curtains in passionate wonder. The movements of my mother's knitting needles, secreting sweaters as they clashed like domesticated fencing foils, held for me the inexhaustible charm of a log fire or the sea, whose ever-changing monotony keeps me hypnotized. And after a few months of war, each day marked off with a furious cross on any calendar I could find, after Ferreira's leg and the death of Corporal Paulo, a primary-school teacher who spent each night, squiffy on wine, giving loud lectures outside the officers' mess, prolix discourses on second-degree equations, surrounded by a pack of ignorant dogs angrily barking in the darkness, I used to spend each evening watching the exhausted stops and starts of the sewing machine and the chief's sharp, piston-rod elbows like those of a racewalker at the end of an excessively long race. When they called me to the radio, the machine had just choked on the second lieutenant's shirt and was coughing up threads and buttons and bits of cloth through various rusty orifices, and the chief, clutching his head, was frantically jumping up and down around that venerable contraption like Buster Keaton with one of his disastrous inventions.

Wait, let me fill your glass. Would you like to suck your slice of orange and spit it out into the ashtray, like a dull, desiccated slice of October sun, would you like to suck your orange slice, eyes lowered, so as to spare yourself the derisory spectacle of my maudlin reaction, the reaction of a drunk at two in the morning when bodies begin to sway back and forth like windshield wipers and the bar becomes a *Titanic* sinking fast, full of silent mouths singing silent hymns, opening and closing like the fat lips of fish? Because there is something of the submerged Spanish galleon about this place, peopled with the floating corpses of crew members bathed in a diagonal, sublunar light, corpses that drift out of their chairs, waving boneless arms like indolent strands of seaweed. Even the waiters become slow, sleepy, putting down roots at the counter like stupefied bits of coral that the barman revives now and then with the smelling salts of a pear brandy, thus saving them from a vegetable coma. And here we are, drowning too, occasionally closing the fans of our eyelids, aquarium octopuses bubbling words that the background music dissolves into a tidal murmur, with you listening to me with the calm patience of a statue (which language would statues use if they could speak, what words do they whisper to the night in the hollow silence of museums, those sarcophagi furnished with spittoons?), yes, with you listening to me, and me telling you about being called to the radio to hear from Gago Coutinho, letter by letter, the news of the birth of my daughter, and me clinging to the back of the radio officer's chair and thinking, Fuck, I'm going to faint.

I got married, you see, four months before I left for Angola, it was on a sunny August afternoon, and my memory of the occasion is confused but intense, the sound of the organ, the flowers on the altar, and the family's tears lent an improbably gentle Buñuelesque touch, and after a few brief weekend encounters, during which we made urgent love, inventing a kind of desperate tenderness full of the anxiety of imminent separation, we said good-bye in the rain, at the dockside, not crying but clinging to each other like orphans. And now, six thousand miles away, my daughter, the fruit of my sperm, whose slow subterranean growth beneath the skin of her mother's belly I did not witness, suddenly burst into the communications hut, among newspaper cuttings and calendars bearing pictures of naked actresses, delivered to me by the stork of that clear voice coming down the line from Gago Coutinho, saying, charlie oscar november golf romeo alpha tango uniform lima alpha tango india oscar november sierra, congratulations from the battalion.

Mille baisers pour ma fille et ma chère petite maman: my grandmother once showed me a piece of paper as fragile as a leaf from an herbarium, the telegram in which my grandfather, during the war in France, responded to my mother's birth, and, as I studied a photograph of a woman and a dog licking each other's parts, I recalled a small, silent man with white hair and a hearing aid, sitting on the verandah of the house in Nelas, staring out at the hills, I remembered those late afternoons in Beira, in September, a long time ago, when the family gathered around me and around my brothers to form a sort of tender, protective reredos, I remembered my mother's smile, which I rarely saw later on, and the creeper that tapped against the window at night, calling on us to perform mysterious Peter Pan–type feats of derring-do. And now, alone, leaning against the wire fence in Chiúme, so that no one would see my tears, leaning against the wire fence in Chiúme and watching how the hill ran down to the plain and looking beyond the plain to the jungle of death in the East, the thin, pale jungle of death in the East, I thought about my unknown daughter lying in a cot in the hospital, among other hospital cots that you could peer at through a porthole, I thought about the daughter whom I had so wanted as a living witness to myself, in the hope that, through her, I might be granted partial redemption for my mistakes, my defects, and my faults, for the failed plans and grandiloquent dreams to which I dared not give form and meaning. Perhaps one day she would write the novels I was afraid to attempt and find for them the exact color and

---

* "A thousand kisses for my daughter and her darling mama."

rhythm, perhaps she would enjoy with other people the close, warm, generous contact that I both wanted and feared, perhaps she and I would achieve a patiently won understanding that would, in a way, justify me, and for which her mother had waited in vain for years. You see, I, too, often let sentimentality stand in for a real desire to change and blithely inflict wounds on other people in the name of that peculiar blend of self-pity and repentance that more often than not disguises a fierce egotism. The lucidity bestowed on me by that second bottle of vodka is so unbearable that, if you don't mind, I'd rather move on to the muted clarity of Cognac, which dyes my inner mediocrity the faint lilac of painful solitude, which at least partly justifies and pardons me. Isn't it the same with you? Don't you ever feel the urge to vomit yourself up? As I grow older and the need to survive becomes less pressing, less urgent, I see myself more clearly than. . . . But here's the Cognac: by the second sip, you'll see, your anxiety will change direction, existence will gradually take on a more pleasant shade, we will slowly begin to appreciate ourselves, to defend ourselves, to be capable of continuing to destroy. With this ninety-proof bandage on my esophagus, I feel free to take up my narrative where I left off a few moments ago: it's 1971, we're in Chiúme, and my daughter has just been born. She has just been born and, at that hour, the ladies of the National Women's Movement must be thinking about us from beneath the Martian helmets of their hair dryers, the patriots of the National Union Party are thinking of us as they buy black, see-through underwear for their secretaries, the Portuguese Youth Movement is thinking of us as they tenderly prepare new heroes to replace us, businessmen are thinking of us as they manufacture modestly priced armaments, the Government is thinking of us as it awards miserable little pensions to the widows of soldiers, and we, wretched ingrates, the target of so much love, either leave our barbed-wire compounds to be killed, out of sheer perversity, by a mine or in an ambush, or we negligently leave behind us fatherless children who will be taught to point at our photo next to the television, in family rooms we have never known. I remember driving into the jungle in a Mercedes truck when one of the men lost his leg to an antipersonnel mine and was still lying there on the sand, conscious and writhing in agony, and I remember how, without a word, small, wrinkled Second Lieutenant Eleutério placed a hand on my shoulder, one of the rare moments in my life when I did not feel alone.

1

*L*et me pay the bill. No, seriously, let me pay and pretend to be the ideal young Portuguese technocrat, circa 1979, someone with the intelligence of the average *Expresso* reader, namely, materialistic, superficial, and inoffensive, with a taste for the kind of books published by, say, Cadernos Dom Quixote, wordy, weird, and rather superficial, the politics of swish bars, restaurants, and resorts, someone who would have in his apartment an etching by Júlio Pomar,* a sculpture by João Cutileiro,† and an old-fashioned phonograph, someone enjoying an emancipated, tortuous relationship full of stormy short circuits with a landscape gardener, who, when she performs the dioptric striptease of taking out her contact lenses at night and placing them in the ashtray, loses the fuzzily charming gaze of those American actresses who appear in

---

* Júlio Pomar (b. 1926) is a celebrated Portugese painter of the neorealist and, later, neo-Expressionist schools.

† João Cutileiro (b. 1937) is a Portuguese sculptor famed for his marble sculptures of female torsos.

Nicholas Ray movies and is transformed instead into boring suburban nakedness, rummaging in her purse for her contraceptive
pills. We should all use suspenders to keep our souls from slipping
down to our heels, Vidalie advised his friends in a bar that May
1968 had left intact, just as, for some reason, the tides leave certain
rocks on the beach untouched, and perhaps that way we would
stop tripping over the trouser bottoms of our most carefully
painted and powdered plans, which always have the most appalling halitosis when viewed from close up. There are few things I
still believe in, and, from three o'clock in the morning on, the
future shrinks to the terrifying proportions of a tunnel through
which I walk, bellowing out the ancient pain I haven't yet managed to cure, as ancient as the death that has been growing its
sticky, febrile moss inside us since infancy, inviting us to embrace
the inertia of the moribund, but there's also the diffuse, volatile,
omnipresent, passionate clarity that you find in Matisse's paintings
and in Lisbon afternoons, which, like the African dust, gets in
through every crack and crevice, through closed windows and the
soft spaces between the buttons on a shirt, through the porous
wall of the eyelids and through silences the texture of murdered
glass, and it's not impossible that the unexpected beauty of a young
woman, who, oblivious to your presence, walks past you in the
restaurant, where the head of the fish on your plate is gazing at you
with imploring, orgasmic eyes, will suddenly awaken in you the
fragile miracle of a pang of desire and happiness. Perhaps it's that
moment of surprise, that unexpected Christmas, that basically
motiveless joy we're both waiting for here, in this bar that we wish
was inhabited by Huck Finn's father and his mad, brilliant drinking bouts, and where we sit as motionless as chameleons waiting

for the fly of an idea, and change color according to the shade of the alcohol we imbibe. Just as I changed color when I went into the bathroom one morning and found the Katangan officer brushing his teeth, his gums, the roof of his mouth, his tongue, and his whole face with my toothbrush.

"*Bonjour, mon lieutenant,*" he gurgled, giving me a vast smile that ran down his chin in pink dribble.

They had arrived in Chiúme some days before, a whole troop of very small black Africans with large heads and red neckerchiefs, whose unruly mustaches gave them the falsely intellectual appearance of saxophonists at the Cascais Jazz Festival, geniuses of the semiquaver whom the diminutive Ben Webster[*] would have excommunicated. They were under the command of a middle-aged second lieutenant who introduced himself as a cousin of Moise Tshombe and spoke French like a Linguaphone record playing at the wrong speed.

"*J'ai très bien connu Mobutu, mon lieutenant,*" he told me, dredging up a gob of spit from the Altamira caves of his lungs, "*il était caporal comptable à l'armée belge.*"[†]

Recruited and armed by the PIDE, they formed an insolent, undisciplined horde labeled by Radio Zambia as "the hired assassins of the Portuguese colonialists": they took no prisoners and returned from the bush screaming and shouting, their pockets stuffed with as many ears as they could cut off; they stole women from the compound right under the nose of the chief, who sat in

---

[*] Ben Webster (1909–1973) was considered one of America's top three jazz tenor saxophonists, along with Coleman Hawkins and Lester Young.

[†] "I knew Mobuto very well, Lieutenant . . . he was a company clerk in the Belgian Army."

resigned despair, ever more lost in contemplation of the landscape before him, leaning one elbow and what remained of his soul on his now definitively broken sewing machine, and looking more and more like a beached whale; they were constantly bristling with the sorts of demands and sulky complaints made by guests at luxury hotels, using threats to spur on the already solicitous staff; they refused to do certain tasks with the arrogance of executives afraid of being mistaken for the concierge; and Tshombe's cousin, undismayed by our expressions of nausea, feasted on barbecued rat and then cleaned his sated teeth with my toothbrush, justifying this with disarming simplicity:

"*Excusez-moi, mon lieutenant, je pensais qu'elle était à tout le monde.*"*

"PIDE has more power than the army," said the chief with a kind of desolate incredulity, pointing to the white civilians who occasionally arrived in order to conspire with the Katangans in some corner of the wire enclosure, shifty-looking individuals whose very amiability boded ill; indeed, once, in the mess in Gago Coutinho, our lieutenant had grabbed their inspector by the throat for calling another officer who wasn't there a coward:

"Get out of here, you bastard."

However, word came from the authoritarian brigadiers at area command that anyone who got into a fight with the patriotic heroes of the Security Forces could expect to run some very unpleasant military risks. The lieutenant burst into my room in a frenzy of indignation:

"They're all sons-of-bitches, Doc, the whole lot of them, and yet we're the ones risking our necks. Can't you come up with some nice

---

* "Excuse me, Lieutenant, I thought it was for everyone."

little disease that would get me out of here because I'm sick to the back teeth of this goddam war."

I was just passing through battalion headquarters on my way to Luanda and leave time in Lisbon. I was lying on my bed after lunch, with the spaghetti I'd eaten weighing like a fetus in my belly.

"Any illness will do, Doc," the lieutenant went on, "anemia, leukemia, rheumatism, cancer, goiter, some little disease, any fucking disease that will get me transferred to the reserves. I mean, what are we doing here? Have you asked yourself what it is we're doing here? Do you think anyone's grateful? No, dammit, they're not! Even worse, yesterday I got a letter from my wife, informing me that the maid just quit, decamped and left: you see what happens when I'm not there to sort her out? Believe me, Doctor, if the master of the house doesn't occasionally stick his ladle in the soup, no maid is ever going to feel any real loyalty to the household. I'd bought her black stockings and red panties, the colors of the artillery, my wife would leave early for work and the maid would bring me breakfast in bed, as good as gold, wearing those stockings and panties, she'd lift up the sheet, take a look and say, 'Ooh, you are big today, sir.' Oh, Doctor, I wish you could have seen her! Such manners! Such delicacy! I never heard a rude word from her, it was always your thingummy this and your doodah that, give me your doodah, sir, I do so like your doodah, put your doodah inside my thingummy sir. *Now* what am I going to do, eh?"

With my eyes closed, with the lieutenant's voice booming around the room, I was thinking: for eleven months now I haven't seen curtains or carpets or wineglasses or asphalt, and it was as if those four absences constituted the elementary basis for any kind of happiness, for eleven months I've seen nothing but death and anxiety and suffering and courage and fear, for eleven months I've masturbated every night, like an adolescent, weaving variations on a theme around the tits in the photographs in the radio hut, for eleven months I haven't known what it is to have a body close to mine or enjoyed a peaceful night's sleep, I have a daughter I've never seen, a wife who is a muffled cry of love in an air letter, friends whose faces I'm inevitably beginning to forget, a house, furnished on credit, that I've never visited, I'm twenty-odd years old, in the middle of my life, and everything seems to be hanging in suspension around me like those people you see in old photographs, frozen in a pose.

"I'm off on the biplane to Luanda tomorrow. Do you want me to give the soup a stir for you?"

And then it was back to the bay, the palm trees, the long-legged white birds, the soldiers' cafés, the men with grubby briefcases on the esplanades changing money at twenty percent, the mulattas swaying their hips, the shoeshine boys, the cripples, the indescribable poverty of the shantytowns, the whores in Bairro Marçal lit obliquely by the headlights of the Jeeps, the guys from the coffee plantations visiting the cabarets on the island and groping the decrepit, frog-eyed dancers there, a pretentious, grimy colonial city that I never liked, greasy with humidity and heat, I hate your streets that go nowhere, your tame Atlantic that smells of detergent, the sweat of your armpits, the strident bad taste of your luxury hotels. I don't belong to you nor you to me, everything about you repels me, I refuse to accept that this is my country, I, a man of so many mingled bloods, with grandparents from all over, Swiss, German, Brazilian, Italian, my country is thirty thousand square miles wide with its center in Benfica in my parents' black bed, my country is where Marshal Saldanha points his finger and the Tagus flows obediently in that direction, it's my aunts' pianos and the specter of Chopin floating in the afternoon on the air rarefied by the breath of visitors, my country, as Ruy Belo[*] wrote, is what the sea rejects.

White birds, trawlers going out to fish just before nightfall. The stewardess who had assigned me my seat on the plane suddenly reappeared while I was struggling with a recalcitrant seatbelt and handed me a folded piece of paper.

"Come and see me when you get back, Blue Eyes."

[*] Ruy Belo (1933–1978) was a Portuguese poet and translator of, among others, Antoine de Saint-Exupéry and García Lorca.

I

_____

At four in the morning, mirrors are still sufficiently merciful or opaque not to reflect back at us our crumpled, shrunken, insomniac face, enlivened only by lifeless, blinking eyes: the excess of light in the airport meant that I didn't have to see in the windows the reflection of my hesitant silhouette bent forward like a rod over the large fish of my suitcase, or my tie, doubtless diverted from the bisecting line of my shirt collar by many hours in a plane and transformed into a limp, melting Dalí clock of a rag, or the lines that had accumulated around my eyes, like the concentric circles of sand in Japanese gardens. The only significant difference between the man returning home alone from the war, walking past clusters of indifferent foreigners, and the two of us heading out of the bar along the corridor formed by backs of heads and profiles whose monotonous diversity bears a close resemblance to shop-window mannequins frozen in pathetically futile gestures, is a few men lying dead along the jungle path, corpses you never knew, that those backs of heads and profiles never saw, and of which the foreigners at the airport were unaware, and that are, therefore, nonexistent, nonexistent, you understand, nonexistent, as nonexistent as your tender feelings for me, as your quick, affectless smile that vanishes almost as soon as it appears, as your motionless hand that passively accepts the touch of my fingers, and your inert thigh against which mine presses so urgently. Your body slips away from me just as, after taking six downers, our own limbs escape us, break free, adopt the sinuous, boneless gestures of octopuses, and your head is full of indecipherable thoughts from which I feel excluded, condemned to remain standing, waiting, on the doormat of your ironic sideways glances, you're a sardine can to which I don't have the key. Do you remember the weekend fishermen along the harbor wall, who used to spend all night casting their happy, stubborn hooks out into the river? Well, if you were slowly to rest your head on my shoulder, if your thigh were to rub against mine until the friction between the two provoked the flinty spark of a contented erection, if you were to look at me, and your eyes were suddenly to grow moist with consent and abandonment, we might perhaps be able to find in ourselves the same barely containable subterranean joy, the same intense, expectant, hopeful pleasure, the same happiness that feeds on itself just as the morning's bright folds devour the scintillating heart of the day. We could grow old together, us and the television, the vertices of a domestic equilateral triangle protected by the tutelary shade of an ornate lampstand and a still life featuring partridges and apples, as melancholy as a blind man's smile, and we could find in the bottle of Drambuie on the sideboard a sugary antidote to the resigned submissiveness of those afflicted by rheumatism. We could rub each other's bony spurs with some herbal balm, take our blood-pressure pills in unison at mealtimes, and on Sundays, after a visit to the cinema, thanks to a big-screen kiss, clasp each other in the spasmodic embrace of newborn babes, breathing heavily through our false teeth like bronchitic kettles. And lying on my back on the orthopedic mattress, which is now little more than a fakir's wooden plank intended to prevent any sciatic twinges, I will remember the ardent, healthy young man I was many years ago, able to eat a second helping of chicken stew without getting heartburn, and for whom the horizon of the future was not limited by the Andean peaks of a threatening electrocardiogram, a young man returning from the war in Africa to meet his daughter for the first time, on one of those November mornings as sad as a rainy school playground during a math lesson.

The female voice, coming from nowhere and announcing in three languages the departure of planes, floated, immaterial, above my head, like a cloud painted by Delvaux, before dissolving gradually into a foam of syllables in which echoed the names of strange cities, San Salvador, La Paz, Buenos Aires, Montevideo, buildings a hundred stories high in which the Adam's apples of elevators are constantly swallowing, going up and down, vomiting out swarthy, mustachioed functionaries whose smiles open like curtains to reveal amiably carnivorous gold teeth. In those vehement countries, where coup d'états and earthquakes succeed each other in a theatrical chain intended (without success) to penetrate the somnambular indifference of a populace of tango fanatics who, ever since Gardel died in that plane crash, have been waiting for a new tango, a new *Cumparsita*, to wake them from their sleep, in such countries I could, poised between a cactus and a woman called Dolores, begin living the generous existence of the Camilo Torres* who lurks inside me, buried, it's true, beneath successive corneal

---

*Father Camilo Torres (1929–1966) was a Roman Catholic priest, Colombian Socialist, and liberation theologian who became a member of the National Liberation Army in Colombia, where he was killed during an ambush.

layers of egotism and laziness, but crying out with passionate indignation. Dozens of Sierra Maestras were just waiting for my beard and my cigar and for me to sit, leaning against the trunk of a tree, calmly solving chess problems and scaring the shit out of paunchy dictators protected by CIA Ray-Bans and chewing gum. The customs officer, a thin, tetchy man who probably suspected I was a guerrilla in the making, sourly and meticulously rummaged around in my suitcase in search of libertarian machine guns.

"I have an eight-month-old fetus hidden among my shirts," I said cheerily, just to increase his irritation and his zeal. He had the disappointed, frenetic look of a man who lies down in bed each night beside a frigid wife kept alive only by the iron lung of the radio soaps.

"You guys come back from Angola thinking you're really big men, but this isn't the jungle here, soldier." And his voice, articulating the words very carefully, as if he had learned his Portuguese from a record, suddenly brought to mind my old Portuguese teacher at school, an exaggeratedly dapper fellow with buffed nails and a signet ring, who used to recite poems by Tomás Ribeiro, standing on the tiptoes of his patent-leather shoes, drawing rapturous, tremulous emotions up from the depths of his esophagus:

> The chatter of magpie and parrot,
> The cackle of laying hen,
> The tender coo-coo of the pigeon,
> The mournful cry of the dove.

"If we were in the jungle, I'd shoot you in the balls."

The elderly bureaucrat ahead of me turned around, looking shocked, one lady said to another, They're all like that when they come back from Africa, poor things, and I felt that everyone was looking at me the way they look at the cripples hauling themselves along on crutches near the Military Hospital, lame frogs—the creation of the Estado Novo's rank stupidity—who, come the evening, would hide the embarrassing stumps of their amputated arms in the sleeves of their sweaters, like ailing pigeons perched on the park benches in the Jardim da Estrela, or could be found in Rua Artilharia Um, where the prostitutes rub their bony asses on the sides of diesel Mercedes cars driven by match-chewing building contractors, horny and sweating beneath their Tyrolean hats. The customs officer, who had taken two horrified steps back, was waiting, pressed against the wall, for me to rake with machine-gun fire the luggage piled up on the counter, and for pants and socks to gush like blood from the bullet holes. The elderly bureaucrat, still shocked, tapped me respectfully on the shoulder and asked:

"Is the fetus in your suitcase in a jar?"

Outside the airport, beneath the night and the rain, stood a line of motionless taxis as solemn as a funeral cortège, and against their dark upholstery I could barely make out the heads of the drivers, who were probably all suffering from the permanent sinusitus of the wretched and the resigned. The halo of light cast by the streetlamps resembled the smoky aureoles above the saints in church paintings, and, as I stared into the deserted, wilting gloom that was gradually fading in an improbable dawn, I thought, So this is Lisbon, and I felt the same incredulous disappointment as when I had visited the house in Nelas many years later, and had found, instead of vast, echoing halls filled by the epic breath of childhood, only small, banal rooms.

Sitting on the back seat of the taxi, with the sound of the ticking meter pulsing like suppressed sobs in my throat, I was trying desperately to recognize my city through those windows covered in pimples of water that slid down the glass, slow as glycerin, but all I could see, in the precarious tremor of the headlights, were the swift profiles of trees and houses that seemed to me swathed in the atmosphere of devout, solitary widowhood that I associate with certain provincial towns when the parish hall isn't showing some pious film bemoaning the lack of candidates for the priesthood. My grandiose memory of a glittering capital city full of movement and mystery straight out of John Dos Passos, which I had been fervently nurturing for a whole year in the sands of Angola, shrank back in shame before those suburban houses in which low-ranking clerks lay snoring amid cheap silver trays and crocheted table linen. A group of men in oilskins were, in waiterly fashion, hosing down the street in the stubborn hope that miraculous chrysanthemums might spring up from the asphalt, like poets of the dawn disguised as deep-sea divers, and the first dogs, as skeletal as El Escorial greyhounds, were trying to sniff out, in the empty frames of doorways, the idea of a bone. Soon, women wearing men's shoes and men wearing no shoes at all would descend from the shacks near the cemetery to look for the meager plunder to be found in the trash, mopping up any food left over in cans or broken bottles: they were like my aunts' "charitable cases," to whom, at Christmas, they would offer, through the parish priest, that demiurge of annual charity, slices of cake, evangelical words, and medicines past their sell-by date, the poor who were always surrounded by screaming, lice-ridden children, like characters out of a Portuguese version of a Vittorio de Sica film.

"What a shithole this country is," I declared to the driver, who responded with a distrustful sideways glance in the rearview mirror that reduced his face to two small, hostile eyes, to which the glass gave a sharp, protuberant, metallic glint. On the dashboard, on either side of a printed notice demanding sharply that any cigarette ends should be placed in a kind of marsupial pouch made of aluminum and stuck like a wart to the back of the front seat, there were two postcards, one showing Our Lady of Fátima and the other St. Thérèse of Lisieux. Oh, no, a brother of Christ, I thought, I'm screwed. And hoping to assuage the crusading indignation of a Catholic, I added loudly: "Christ be praised," trying to imitate the majestic Beira accent of the cardinal patriarchs, whose slow, thurible gestures conceal the ossified suspicions of a peasant still wary of trains.

"Trains always make me dream," I said as I stood outside the old front door flanked by stone pineapples: the man gazed at me, incredulous and amazed, quite forgetting about the money I owed him and looking as surprised as if Christmas had fallen in November.

The street, Travessa do Vintém das Escolas, the tall façade of the house, the courtyard of the tanning factory in which a desperate dog kept up a constant barking, the rainy, milky sky, the bare branches of the bougainvillea against the wall: I've arrived, I'm going to go up the stairs, dragging my suitcase behind me, I'm going to open the door, walk in, and dissolve into your arms that have been alone for so long; lying beside you, I'm going to watch the day dawning through the narrow skylight and listen for the angelic arrival of the baker, I'm going to touch your skin, your legs, the soft, tender hollow between your thighs, the bright space that separates your breasts and has the mother-of-pearl sheen of certain secret shells that the low tide exhibits as proudly as if they were treasures, I'm going to enter you slowly, deeply, supporting myself on my hands so that I can see you when you give your joyful orgasmic shout, with your head, surrounded by an ellipse of curly hair, rolling from side to side on the pillow, your eyes suddenly blind, suddenly opaque, cast into darkness by the trembling paramecium fringe of your eyelashes. It's difficult to talk about this while standing next to the bar's doorman, who somehow manages to be simultaneously intransigent and obsequious and demands a tip with the peremptory subservience of an armed assailant, proffering me the braided sleeve of his jacket the way the elephant at the zoo reaches out his soft trunk for the bunch of carrots brought by his keeper. It's awkward, you see, especially since I can't find a single coin in my pocket to satisfy the authoritarian appetites of this creature who is beginning to frown now with the frank hostility of all large, irate beasts, ready, in the grip of a primeval pachydermal rage, to trample me with the enormous soles of his shoes and transform my arms into elaborate Art Nouveau arabesques like the judiciously rusty arms of the chandeliers, whose bright bulbs strike glittering lunar lights from the bald pates beneath. And so I climbed the stairs, dragging behind me the awkward tail of my suitcase and conscious of an explosive knot of tears in my throat, and I found a woman in bed and a baby in a cot, both sleeping in the same defenseless pose, fragile and abandoned, and I stood there in the room, my head still full of the echoes of war, the sound of gunfire and the indignant silence of the dead, listening, you understand, to the sounds formed by the complex web of breaths, then I noticed one of my wife's ankles was sticking out from beneath the sheets and I began stroking it until she woke, wordlessly pulled back the covers, and received me, entire, into the warm hollow of the bed. The lieutenant's voice was booming out from far, far away, Give your missus a bang, give your missus a bang, give your missus a bang, that's what you have to do, Doctor, the captains promoted from sergeants would be play-

ing checkers in the mess in Luso, Ferreira's stump would be heal-
ing, the stump of the leg he no longer had, and I felt as if I were
making love on behalf of all of them, you see, avenging all their
suffering and anxiety as I entered that body, which opened to me
like a night flower, then closed slowly around my exhausted
flanks.

Perhaps one day, if we get to know each other better, I'll show
you the photo in my wallet of my green-eyed daughter whose eyes
change when she cries and become the color of a wild equinoctial
sea leaping the seawall in an angry crochet of foam, I'll show you
her smile, her mouth, her fair hair, the daughter I dreamed about for
nine months in the sweaty heat of Angola, because, as Luandino*
used to say, we are the only ones who truly exist, and all the rest is
a lie, we are the only ones who truly exist, she and I, her long body,
her hands so like mine, the indefatigable curiosity of her questions,
her anxious concern if I'm silent or sad, we are the only ones who
truly exist and all the rest is a lie, I'll show you the serious expression on my daughter's face, the daughter I didn't watch growing in
her mother's swollen belly, the daughter for whom I was just a photograph to be pointed at and who gave me the angry reception all
intruders deserve, back from Angola lying with her in my arms for
whole afternoons on end, exchanging the wise, ancient, knowing
smiles that all four-month-old babies inherit from albums and take
years and years to lose, He's having a nap, and I don't want you to
wake him up, I said to the soldiers, the chaplain paced around the
coffin, tracing crosses in the air with his fingers, the lieutenant muttered Fucking war fucking war fucking war, I'm a civilian again for

*José Luandino Vieira (b. 1935), an Angolan writer of short fiction and novels,
was deeply committed to the struggle for Angolan independence from Portugal.

a few days and I'm traveling the gentle geography of your body, the river of your voice, the cool shade of your hands, the pigeon-breast down of your pubis, but me and Xana and you, the Saturday rain, we are the only ones who truly exist, the sudden crying of our daughter waking us in the dark in our tangled sheets, the baby's bottles warmed up in the kitchen on nights of anguish and hope, but when I go to bed now, you understand, the future is a thick fog over a Tagus empty of boats, just the occasional distressed cry in the mist, I will live for a long time in your gestures, my daughter. The family came to visit me like curious onlookers watching from a safe distance an earthquake, a landslide, a suicide, a disaster, a man lying facedown on the ground beside a smashed car, an epileptic flailing around on the pavement, a heart-attack victim clutching his chest in the grocer's store, the grave lines on my father's face, my uncles' jokes, the drunken speeches of Corporal Paulo who was blown up by a mine, and suddenly there was the plane taking me back to Angola, my wife leaning against a pillar, not saying a word, and me with all the saliva in my mouth dried up, you know how it is, my tongue as dry as a chicken's, the lights of my city seen from above: I watched the Boeing you were traveling in from the departure-lounge window, she wrote, and I felt such a pang.

M

So what's it to be, your place or mine? I live in Picheleira, behind the Fonte Luminosa, in an apartment with a view of the river, the far side of the estuary, the bridge, and the city at night, like one of those foldout panoramic views for tourists, and whenever I arrive and open the front door and cough, the far end of the corridor returns my cough as an echo and that gives me a really odd feeling, you know, as if I were about to meet myself in the blind mirror in the bathroom, where a sad smile awaits me, hanging from my face like a garland worn during a Carnival long since over. Have you ever noticed how, when you're alone, your gestures become uncoordinated, unharmonious, orphaned, how your eyes search for some impossible companionship in their own reflection and your polka-dot tie gives you the derisory appearance of a poor clown going through the motions of a pathetically unfunny act for the benefit of an empty circus? At times like that, I usually sit on the floor in my daughters' bedroom, they come and visit me once every two weeks, you see, scattering crumbs and trading cards around the other empty rooms, and I watch over their sleep with genuine solicitude, stumbling over the legs of dolls, comic books, and plastic cradles that are arranged on the carpet according to a mysterious code that I struggle to crack in their absence, just as we do when we look at photos of the dead and search our memories for fugitive expressions too fluid for photos to capture and that slip through their fingers. On Tuesdays and Fridays, a woman from Cape Verde comes, I've never seen her and we communicate via polite messages that we leave stuck on the door of the kitchen cupboard, anyway, she restores all the objects and furniture to the excessively geometric order of solitude, on which the lack of dust confers the aseptic impersonality of a surgical supply room, and she pins out on the balcony my monotonous men's clothes without a single bra to spice them up with a suggestion of conjugal bliss. From time to time, I might meet a woman by chance on a sofa at some gathering of friends, the way you might find odd bits of change in the pocket of a winter coat, and she'll come up with me in the elevator in order to do a brief imitation of attraction and tenderness that I know down to its smallest details, from the initial brazen whisky to the amorous glance that lasts just long enough for me to know it's not real, to the moment when love ends in a quick splash in the bidet, where all great effusions vanish with a little soap, rage, and warm water. We say good-bye in the hall, exchange phone numbers that are immediately forgotten and a disappointed kiss that the lack of lipstick drains of all color, and then she evaporates from my life, leaving on the sheet a stain like egg white that constitutes the white seal certifying that love is officially over: all that's left is a strange perfume that coats my armpits with a vaguely whorish smell and a smear of makeup on my throat, which I discover the next morning while performing the bloody hara-kiri of shaving, and those two things confirm the brief sojourn in my bed of someone I had already assumed to be a vague invention of my melancholia. Meanwhile, one by one, the faucets and the cistern stop working, the blinds get stuck like complicated eyelids that refuse to open, the humidity cultivates converging islands of mold in the wardrobes; slowly, insidiously, the apartment is dying; from its open mouth comes an air redolent of spent breath, the molten pupils of the lightbulbs stare at me in a final, anguished mist; seated at my desk, I feel as if I were on the deserted bridge of a sinking ship, with its books, its plants, its unfinished manuscripts, its nonexistent curtains buffeted by the pale wind of an obscure happiness. The block being built opposite me will soon wall me in as if I were a character out of a story by Poe and only my teeth will be visible, glittering in the darkness, like those of ancient skeletons crouched in the corner of a cave, embracing their bony knees with the yellowing tendons of their elbows.

And how do *you* manage? I imagine you inhabiting some zone halfway between Oriental philosophy and the thoughtful, lucid Left, for whom May 1968 represented a kind of irritating childhood illness that reduced the dream to the disenchanted, utilitarian, cynical Marxism of certain Eastern European bureaucracies: a lot of cushions on the floor, a smell of incense and patchouli, various Indian knickknacks, a Siamese cat as disdainful as a prima donna, books by Reich[*] and Garaudy,[†] who continue their passionate prophetic monologues on your shelves, the voice of Léo Ferré[‡] emerging in spirals of febrile passion from the record player. Mustachioed, artfully unkempt architects occasionally occupy your antique,

---

[*] Wilhelm Reich (1897–1957) was one of the most radical figures in the history of psychiatry. He tried to reconcile Marxism with psychoanalysis.

[†] Roger Garaudy (b. 1913), a prominent philosopher, converted to Islam in 1982. His controversial book, *The Founding Myths of Modern Israel*, led to his trial in France for Holocaust denial.

[‡] *Léo Ferré (1916–1993) was a French poet, composer, singer, and musician.

wrought-iron bed bought in Sintra and fill your designer ashtrays with unfiltered cigarette butts or stroke their hairy chests as they discourse on the shape of supermarkets to come. In the morning, the fat, surly concierge brings in the trash cans, her bulldog brows beaming out silent insults. From the apartment next door come the furious gibes of a marital argument, accompanied by the sound of crockery being broken. A sun as cheerful as the smile on a policeman's face plays xylophone on the shutters. In your slippers, in the kitchen, you prepare the electric shock of some strong coffee that will catapult you out of your envelope of sleep toward work, at the wheel of a cream Renault 4 with the trunk smashed in by some angry taxi driver. Inhabitants of the same city, we have spent years and years walking past each other without even noticing, we go to the same cinemas, we read the same newspapers, we regularly watch the TV soaps with the same mixture of fascination and irritation. We are, if I may put it like this, contemporaries, and our parallel trajectories will finally meet in my apartment (because the smell of incense makes me nauseous) with all the limp joy of two strands of spaghetti entwining. Shall I turn on the car radio? It's always possible that the three o'clock bulletin will announce the resurrection of the flesh and that we'll reach Benfica Cemetery in time to see, emerging from the family vault, all those ladies from the old photos with their parasols and intriguingly vast bosoms. What? The war in Africa? Yes, you're right, I am getting off the point, like an old man on a garden bench lost in the strange labyrinth of the past, mulling over memories amid marble busts and pigeons, his pockets full of stamps and toothpicks and dominoes, and constantly grinding his teeth as if he were about to launch some definitive, extraordinary gob of spit. The truth, you see, is that, as Lisbon moved farther away from me, my country was becoming unreal, my country, my home, my clear-eyed daughter in her cradle, were all becoming as unreal as these trees, these façades, these dead streets that, in the absence of light, resemble a defunct fair, because Lisbon, you understand, is a provincial fairground, a traveling circus that has pitched camp by the river, a fantasy in ceramic tiles that repeat themselves, attracting and repelling, their hesitant colors fading into geometric rectangles on the sidewalks, no, seriously, we live in a country that doesn't exist, there's absolutely no point in looking for it on the maps because it doesn't exist, there's a round dot, a name, but that's not it, Lisbon only starts to take shape in the distance, to take on depth and life and vibration. Mist-bound Luanda rose to meet me, and I stepped off the plane bent double beneath the weight of thirty-five days of anguish and joy, repeating to myself *Surtout pas d'émotion*, as Blondin advised, repeating with every step, *Surtout pas d'émotion, Surtout pas d'émotion, Surtout pas d'émotion,** my hotel window opened onto the confused morning of Mutamba, I took the photograph of my daughter out of the suitcase and placed it between the telephone and the glass of water in that anonymous room smelling of disinfectant, Formica, and rubber, then lay down on the bedspread fully clothed and with my shoes still on, and when the single glass tulip of the ceiling lamp became two, I fell asleep.

The night arrives too suddenly in the tropics, after a twilight as fleeting and bland as the kiss shared by a couple divorced by mutual consent. The palm trees along the bay waved the feathers of their leaves in lazy flutterings, the trawlers left the harbor, belching out their dinner of diesel, the neon lights on the island's nightclubs winked painted eyelids, sending out eager calls in which I heard an echo of the women in charge of the rifle ranges in Parque Mayer,

---

* "Above all, not a flicker of fear."

whose hoarse voices peopled my adolescent dreams with a terrify-ing cawing. The heat clothed our gestures in sticky cotton batting, and the water boiled and whistled in the pipes like a geyser. I dined alone in a restaurant downtown, full of sleek, plump men, their necks as shiny as those of Minho oxen, their fingers covered in rings with red or black stones, men who dipped their mustaches into their soup like starving otters. A hunchbacked African was going from table to table trying without success to sell crudely carved dolls that looked more like plastic than wood, until the waiter shooed him out with the napkin he had draped over his shoulder, as black with stains and soot as a snuff handkerchief. A bald old man, with a face like a gargoyle, was devouring a mulatto woman, who, protected from his furious attentions by three strands of necklaces, was, meanwhile, feasting on a vast ice cream, a monster of crystal-lized fruit and cream, topped by an obscene maraschino cherry. A jukebox was vomiting out squealing, paranoid *pasodobles* more suited to a workingman's club, and against this deafening backdrop of bullfighting talk, which was forcing me to scream down the phone as if I were in the dentist's chair, I called the stewardess, who was waiting for me, whisky in hand, in a third-floor apartment in Bairro Prenda, wearing jeans so tight that you could almost see the beating veins in her thighs. A tiny dog, rather like a skinny, long-legged rat, rigid with peevish hostility, came snapping furiously around my ankles, and I considered kidnapping it and giving it to the Katangan lieutenant for his Sunday breakfast, with the kind intention of varying his diet. The young woman picked up the dog by one leg and hurled him into the kitchen, where the creature landed with a shrill yelp that spoke of multiple fractures, then she kicked the door shut: her next move would probably be to crush my balls with a martial-arts thrust of the knee, and the following day they would find my body, horribly mutilated, amid a lot of over-turned furniture and broken bottles.

"Hello, Modesty Blaise,"* I said, shrinking back. Beneath her print T-shirt, her breasts resembled two enormous pears covered by a paper Coca-Cola napkin: without her uniform, she lost the coefficient of mystery that I stubbornly attribute to all angels—a leftover from the catechism—even those who walk down the aisle of a plane serving plastic meals. The apartment smelled of dirty washing and canned dog food, the barn-breath of the African night wafted in through the window, on the unmade bed, a book of poems by Eluard† was a sudden promise that a horizon of fragile, unsuspected sweetnesses might yet exist in that violent Amazon fallen from who-knows-what heaven and who was under orders to break the spinal columns of irritating lapdogs and pulverize the timid testicles of warriors passing through on their way to barbed wire and death, poor uniformed creatures hiding away in the wooden cages of the barracks.

"What'll you have, Blue Eyes?" she asked with a carnivorous smile like an accordion opening that brought to mind my child-hood copy of *Little Red Riding Hood*, full of frightening images: All the better to eat you with, my dear, said the wolf, sitting tucked up in bed and wearing a nightcap but revealing a drooling, sharp-toothed smile.

All the better to eat you with, my dear, all the better to eat you with, my dear, all the better to eat you with, my dear: her mouth

---

* *Modesty Blaise* is a British comic strip whose eponymous heroine is a very tough and intelligent young woman with many talents and a criminal past.

† Paul Eluard (1895–1952), French poet, one of the founders of the surrealist movement.

was growing in my direction, concave, gigantic, bottomless, her red nails were getting longer and longer until they grazed my skin, the chilling smell of raw meat moved closer, her esophagus was a cave, a well, into which the pebble of my body would drop and fall as far as the denim root of her thighs. The tiny dog was scratching at the kitchen door, uttering melancholy whimpers. I put my glass on a bamboo table on which the navel of a Pantagruelian Buddha shook with ceramic laughter, and the clink of ice cubes reminded me of the bell I'd bought for my daughter's cradle that strummed a slow, disconnected tune: at that hour, at home, my wife would be warming up our child's midnight bottle, a cigarette would be burning out in the tin ashtray, sending up serene blue coils of smoke like a censer, the comfort of domestic silences smoothed the rough edges of despair, an eternity like a medieval tableau conjured up images of plump angels painted on the ceiling. Perhaps the sofa in the living room still preserved the fleeting imprint of my buttocks, and perhaps a dilute remnant of my existence still floated in the empty water of the mirrors, lifeless pupils that forget even themselves. In my absence, a whole universe, from which I found myself cruelly excluded, was carrying on imperturbably, its modest pace set by the little panting heart of the alarm clock and by a faucet somewhere, dripping its perpetual drop of sweat in the darkness. The young woman shoved the book off the bed (*larmes des yeux, les malheurs des malheureux*)[*] like someone brushing breadcrumbs from a tablecloth, before sliding, naked, out of her clothes, shaking the mane of her long hair like a great eager mare in heat, and blowing out a kind of steam from her flared nostrils. In Lisbon, my daughter, eyes closed, would be sucking on her bottle, and her ears, in the

---

[*] ". . . tears fall from eyes, misfortunes of the unfortunate . . ."

lamplight, would take on the pink transparency of an Antonioni*
sea, all delicate folds and curves. I took off my pants, unbuttoned
my shirt, the Buddha's navel mocked my pale, troubled thinness, I
lay down on the bed, ashamed of the size of my shriveled penis that
refused to grow, like a wrinkled piece of tripe among the reddish
hairs down below, my hostess politely picked it up with two fingers
as if she were at a formal dinner, and I couldn't tell whether she felt
surprise or disgust, Get hard, you bastard, I told myself, my daughter stopped drinking in order to burp and her unfocused eyes turned
inward, I touched the young woman's vulva and it was soft and
warm and tender and moist, I found the hard nerve of her clitoris
and she gave a sigh like a kettle through the pouting beak of her
lips, For Chrissake, get hard, I begged, shooting a downward glance
at my dead willy, Don't embarrass me like this, get hard, for your
own sake, get hard, go on, dammit, get hard, my wife was changing diapers, a safety pin gripped between her lips, the lieutenant
was probably explaining about his maid to the terrified chaplain,
who kept crossing himself, the coffins in the depot were waiting for
me to lie down in them obediently, in that lead lining, the young
woman stopped kissing me, sat up and leaned on one elbow like a
figure on an Etruscan tomb, stroked my face, and asked, What's
wrong, Blue Eyes? and I shrugged, rolled over onto my stomach,
and burst into sobs.

* Michelangelo Antonioni (1912–2007) was an Italian movie director whose work
included *The Red Desert*, *Blow-Up*, and *Zabriskie Point*.

N

After racing frantically across the tarmac, flapping its wings in desperate, asthmatic pursuit of the air it needed, the Nord Atlas lifted awkwardly off the runway in the clumsy, lopsided flight of a partridge, brushing with its fat, feathered underbelly the corrugated iron roofs of the shantytowns, where men and dogs in their misery were suffocating in the steamy, bleach-scented heat. We sat squashed together on the one long bench in the plane, among crates, bundles, bags, and suitcases ("my country scattered on the ground in Gare d'Austerlitz"): a forced emigré thanks to the war, I was on my way back to my own wire-fenced shantytown, and looking out of the narrow windows of the plane, I saw how the island of Luanda gradually shrank in the distance, saw the city grow suddenly insubstantial and small, saw the glassy sea of the bay, the miniature twisting streets intersecting and overlaying each other like eels in a basket, even Bairro Prenda, the scene of my abject failure, where that ghastly dog was probably sitting on the unstained sheet, howling with joy; in the end, I'd hidden away my shame in my underpants in the early hours of the morning, watched by the young woman, who observed me with a mixture of amusement and pity, and then slipped sideways into the elevator like a disenchanted stowaway escaping from a ship before it even left dock, until a taxi scooped up what remained of me and carried me off to my hotel in Mutamba, where the milky neon sign twitched on and off like the final death throes of a snake. The huge black woman sitting nodding in the foyer in front of the key rack raised one indifferent, hippopotamus eyelid in which I thought I glimpsed a fleeting glint of sarcasm. And when I went into the room, I felt like spitting out into the glass of water the coral-pink dentures that might have made my failure more acceptable and less painful, but my teeth remained stubbornly anchored in my gums, and my forehead, when I looked in the mirror, was as yet unlined, and I would probably reach the year 2000 with my prostate in reasonable working order and with enough of a future left in which to cultivate a little hope. And so I closed the window, pulled down the blinds, and began mentally telling the ceiling light the story of the hopeless shipwreck victim I sometimes felt myself to be.

There were nearly twenty of us soldiers heading back east, sitting on the wooden bench, silently smoking, our faces empty of expression, like those images from photo booths in which the eyes show not a hint of emotion, and I realized that I'd lived in that barbed-wire compound with the same men for a whole year but I didn't even know them, we ate the same food and slept the same broken sleep interrupted by fear and cold sweats, bound together by the strange sense of solidarity that binds together patients in hospital wards, a feeling that combines a panicky dread of death and a fierce envy of those outside who carry on the carefree, threatless daily life to which all of us desperately want to return and thus escape from the absurd paralysis imposed by suffering, yes, I had spent a whole year living with the same men and yet we knew nothing about each other, we were incapable of deciphering anything in our mutually hollow eyes, because the face with which one set out into the jungle was always the same face one brought back, only more crumpled and covered by a green moss of beard, our voices had the anonymous neutrality of intercoms, our rare smiles were, as Lewis Carroll put it, like the flames on candles when the flame has gone out, our bodies lying in our bunks might have been hastily mass-produced from the same gray mold, except that the manufacturers had forgotten to include in our muscles' repertoire of movements any sudden gestures of joy.

Gradually, the wear and tear of war, the never-changing land-scape of sand and sparse woods, the long, sad months of mist that turned the sky and the night the sepia brown of faded daguerreo-types, had transformed us into a species of apathetic insect, machines made to withstand a day-to-day existence filled with hopeless hope, afternoons spent sitting on barrel-stave chairs or on the steps of the former administration post, staring at the exces-sively lethargic calendars on which the months lingered with mad-dening slowness, while endless leap days, full of hours, swelled up around us like great bloated, putrefying bellies that kept us impris-oned with no hope of salvation. We were fish, you see, in aquari-ums of cloth and metal, dumb fish, simultaneously fierce and tame, trained to die without protest, to lie down without protest in those army coffins, where we would be welded in, covered with the national flag, and sent back to Europe in the hold of a ship, our dog tags over our mouths to quash even the desire to utter a rebellious scream. The other soldiers watched me return to Chiúme without a flicker of surprise, and not a single officer looked up from his lunch when I sat down with them to eat, between the captain and the Katangan lieutenant, who smiled at everyone but received no response, not even the cruel guffaw of those stone lions you see flanking the kinds of buildings that win architecture prizes. Second Lieutenant Eleutério's cassette was playing Beethoven's Fourth Symphony, and it was as if the music were echoing around an empty room beyond whose curtainless windows the plain endlessly unfolded, a music that continued to exist in its own echo just as in closed pianos the faint rhythms of an ancient waltz still live on, as old and hesitant as the wall clocks in the corridor. We were fish, we are fish, we were always fish, caught between two currents in our search for an impossible compromise between rebellion and resignation, born under the sign of the Portuguese Youth Movement and its stupid, cheap, trenchant brand of patriotism, nourished culturally by the Beira-Baixa railroad line, the rivers of Mozambique, and the Galaico-Duriense Massif, spied on by the thousand ferocious eyes of the PIDE, condemned to read newspapers that the censors reduced to glum, provincial, pious hymns of praise for the Estado Novo, and then flung at last into the paranoiac violence of war, to the sound of martial music and heroic speeches given by those who stayed behind in Lisbon valiantly doing battle against Communism from the safety of church halls, while we, the fish, were dying one by one in that asshole of the world, touch a trip wire and a grenade flies up at you and splits you in two, the nurse sitting on the path staring in astonishment at the sight of his own intestines in his hands, a plump, yellow, disgusting thing hot in his hands, beside him the machine gunner with a hole in his neck continuing to fire, you arrived in Angola not wanting to fight anyone, crippled with fear, but after the first few losses, you went out into the jungle feeling angry, wanting to avenge Ferreira's leg and Macaco's limp and suddenly boneless body, our only prisoners were old men and skeletal women too feeble to escape, concave with hunger, the MPLA left messages on the trails and tracks urging us to desert, but where to, when there was only sand all around, Why don't you desert, they said, they crossed over from Zambia and into the interior, stopping now and then to dynamite the bridges over the rivers, one day, after an attack, I found the MPLA's metal insignia on the runway and I stared at it just as Lourenço was staring at the guts spilling out of his stomach, the corporal showed me a letter he had found on a bush, "I would love to show you my entire body," some Englishwoman had written to an Angolan who had been machine-gunning us the night before, hidden in the shadows, Czech light arms that made a sharp, rapid sound, some Swedish doctors were working in Chalala Nengo, a few kilometers from us, the same Chalala Nengo that the T-6s were bombarding with napalm. One of these mornings, my friends, you'll wake up in a good mood and march over there in a trice and kill the whole lot of them, said the optimistic colonel in starched camouflage who had come from Luanda to encourage us with kind words, advice, and threats, Only if you go first, you stupid bastard, muttered the lieutenant under his breath, If you want a better posting, then you're going to have to give us some visible results, mines, prisoners, explosives, the commander, small, ridiculous, almost touching in his embarrassment, suddenly acquired a nervous tic, repeatedly shrugging his shoulders, as he indicated on the map the area we were responsible for, But Colonel, he stammered, Colonel Colonel Colonel, an area almost half the size of Portugal being defended by five hundred men expected to survive on near-putrid fish, gamy meat, and chicken bones, men worn down by malaria and exhaustion, drinking the muddy water that drip-dripped from the filters, there was no more beer no more cigarettes no more matches, even in Luso there weren't any matches, One morning, my friends, you'll wake

up in a good mood and carry all before you, and the sooner the better because you've achieved very little so far, the commander,
crushed, was turning his cap round and round in his hands, I
wouldn't be surprised if the stupid bastard didn't burst into tears in
front of that fool, muttered the lieutenant, I'm sick to the back teeth
of this goddam war, can't you come up with some nice little disease
for me, Why don't you desert, cried the pamphlets left by the MPLA,
Desert Desert Desert Desert Desert DESERT, the announcer on
Radio Zambia addressed the Portuguese soldiers and asked Why
are you fighting your brothers, but it was ourselves we were fighting, our guns were turned on ourselves, I would love to show you
my body, and I had again already forgotten your body lying with
thighs spread in the attic room where I lived for a month, forgotten
the smell and taste of the soft elasticity of your skin, I had already
forgotten the sound of your voice your smile your tender ironic
Egyptian eyes your large breasts your hair on the pillow your perfect toes, the captain came back from the jungle with a Kalashnikov
under his arm and said The guy was guarding the crops he had his
back to us didn't even see us coming, tomorrow we'll wake up in a
good mood and win the war, Viva Portugal, what does it matter if
the mist seeps right into our bones if Angola-is-ours and the ladies
of the National Women's Movement are all eagerly watching our
progress, here you are, have a few air letters and piss off, do you
know what it's like wanting to make love but having no one to
make love to, the misery of having to masturbate not thinking of
anything, jiggling your foreskin up and down until finally a kind of
feeble fainting fit a little spurt of liquid and that's that wipe your
fingers on your pants, zip up your fly and off to the parade ground,
Slow march and at ease, cadets, ordered the second lieutenant in
charge of drill at Mafra, that absurd monstrous cretinous idiotic

monastery, Ladies and gentlemen sorry officers the Vera Cruz orchestra with our vocalist Tó Mané wish you all a pleasant evening, the guy at the microphone played dusty out-of-tune boleros from old 78s his long hair slick with gloss, the sapper swung his chair around to the chaplain grinned and asked Would you care to dance, the first antivehicle mine exploded in the middle of one of his patrols and I went into the jungle in the helicopter to pick up the wounded, Doctor and blood doctor and blood doctor and blood said the radio, donors in a line with their sleeves rolled up at the entrance to the post, the injured lying motionless on stretchers their eyes closed breathing softly through one corner of their mouth, at night the wild dogs used to bark outside the barbed-wire compound Can you hear them whispered the lieutenant and his breath was hot on my ear, there were no matches so we had to light up using someone else's cigarette, Show us some visible results said the colonel and all we had to show were amputated legs coffins hepatitis malaria corpses vehicles transformed into wrecked harmoniums, the general phoned from Luso to say, Those Berliet trucks are expensive, go over the route first with a fine-tooth comb, so three men on either side tested out the sand ahead of the trucks because a truck was more important and more expensive than a man, you can make a child in five minutes and for free whereas a vehicle takes weeks and months of tightening screws, besides there were still loads of people back home who could be sent to Angola even if you excluded the children of VIPs and the friends of the mistresses of the VIPs who would never ever be sent, the faggy son of a minister was declared psychologically unsuited to the army Can you hear them whispered the lieutenant pointing into the shadows, My love here I am again in Chiúme the journey was fine and everything here is just the same a bit isolated but quiet it's rather like spending two years in Vila Real or Espinho really or on a farm in the Alentejo with the advantage that I'll be able to tell our daughter that I spoke to zebras and elephants in zebraese and elephantese, every evening I would write ridiculous, jocular lies to a disembodied woman, with your color photo in my pocket, a photo of you sitting, legs crossed, on a rock by the sea with your short hair and dark glasses and wearing a red print dress, and it both is you and isn't you, who is it in the photograph smiling at me (at me?), Angola-is-ours, Mr. President and Viva Portugal, we are of course, and passionately proud to be so, the legitimate descendants of Magellan and Cabral and Da Gama and the glorious mission we have been given is as Mr. President has just said in his remarkable speech a very similar one, all we lack are the gray beards and the scurvy but the way things are going well strike me blind if we won't get there, but if you don't mind my asking why is it that the sons of your ministers and your eunuchs, of your eunuch ministers and your minister eunuchs, your minieuchs and your eunisters aren't stuck here in the sand with us, the captain leaned the Kalashnikov against the wall and we stood looking at it in surprise, Is this what our death looks like asked a second lieutenant, Doctor, you're needed, someone had stepped on an antipersonnel mine on the path, we drove three miles in the Mercedes truck as fast as we could and found the squad in a clearing with Corporal Paulo lying on the ground moaning with nothing below his knee but a mangled bloody pulp, nothing else mister president and messieurs eunuchs, nothing, imagine mister president what it would be like to suddenly lose a part of yourself, yes, the legitimate descendants of Cabral and Da Gama disappearing in fractions an ankle an arm a length of intestine your balls your beloved balls blown away, he died in combat the newspaper says but this is what it really means to die you sons-of-bitches, I helped them to die with my useless drugs and their eyes were protesting protesting they didn't understand and they were protesting, is this what dying is, this look of surprise the gaping mouth the limp arms, they covered up the napalm bombs with oilcloth and the government stated solemnly We would never stoop to such cruel methods of extermination, but I saw them covering over the bombs in Gago Coutinho, I asked the nurse for a tourniquet, then remembered Whenever I use a tourniquet they die of a great big embolism in Luso and so I started to look for an artery I could clamp, a medic was peering over my shoulder like a boy from behind the safety of a wall, it was hard to clamp the artery in the middle of all that muscle and blood, what's your body like what's your smile like what's your hair on the pillow like you used to wake me in the morning with hot toast and your thighs between mine and when you walked your buttocks made me mad with desire the way you moved your hips the slow way you kissed Dear Mom and Dad here in Chiúme things are going as well as they possibly could go, possibly, there's no reason at all for you to worry about me I've even put on a pound or two since I arrived and I'm beginning to look like an Irish missionary or a Welsh rugby player, the chief was stroking his useless sewing machine and gazing at it with the eyes of a sorrowful Pietà, the hawks flew over the chickens in the yard in slow, sly, greedy circles, thunderclouds were gathering over the plain, the tendons of the wind contracted and expanded, whistling over the sand, the chief's Mississippi paddle steamer was growing brown with decorative rust, I applied a thick compress to the stump to stanch the blood, the medic was retching and clinging to his gun, for we clung to our rifles as drowning men do to risibly small pieces of wood, Is that what our death looks like, asked the lieutenant, pointing at the Kalashnikov by the wall, our death is these scrawny bushes and this ashen-faced man lying here, delirious, the commander of the troop hissed furiously, Dear Dr. Salazar if you were here and alive I would stick a hand grenade up your ass, take the pin out of a hand grenade and stick it up your ass, I injected a second ampule of morphine into the deltoid muscle, After all my hard work don't go and die on me, from Chiúme they told us that the helicopter had left Gago Coutinho with more blood on board, I love you I love your hands full of rings and your skinny legs that coil about mine like necklaces wound round and round, I like playing cards with you in our unmade bed and the way we both cheat in order to win, one day I'll take a photograph of myself and you'll be amazed how fat I've gotten, two Coramine tablets and three Sympatol in the hope that I won't lose the pulse as rapid and tenuous beneath my fingers as a bird's heart, Slow march and at ease panted the second lieutenant on the Ericeira Road, a line of exhausted cadets on either side of the tarmac beneath the icy March rain, the Vera Cruz orchestra wishes you all a pleasant evening, there's no reason at all to worry about me because this mangled leg isn't yet my leg and so I continue if I can put it like this more or less alive, the colonel in Luanda must have complained to the brigadier that we were dying too much, the helicopter disappeared above the jungle toctoctoctoctoctoc, we got up to leave, we picked up the canvas sheets the cartridge belts the canteens and the rucksacks, the platoon formed up in a line and we noticed during the head count that the vomiting medic was missing, he was sitting close by on a G3 rifle, his chin in his hands, I called him, called him again, and ended up shaking him by the shoulder, he raised somnambulant eyes to me, as if looking at me from a great distance, and then said in a soft childish voice Don't bother about me I'm sick to death of this war and there's no way I'm going to get out of here.

0

$\mathcal{L}$isbon, even at this hour, is a city as devoid of mystery as a nudist beach, where the all-revealing sun brutally exposes flaccid buttocks and flat, shadowless breasts, and which the sea appears to abandon on the sand like smooth pebbles left by the retreating tide. The night—which resembles a notary's office where resigned third-rank civil servants lie snoring among the sheaves of official papers—transforms the houses and the buildings into sad family vaults inhabited by peevish couples who forget their minuscule disputes for a few hours and become like recumbent statues wearing striped pajamas and whom the alarm clock on the bedside table will soon propel back into their gray, frenetic, day-to-day lives. In Parque Eduardo VII, the homosexuals emerge out of the darkness at the approach of cars and stand among the bushes making undulating, jellyfish gestures and fluttering myopic eyes filled with dubious promises and underlined by an excess of mascara. On the other side of the road, as yet uninvaded by the decaying smiles of the prostitutes who share with the insects the shower of pale light from the streetlights, the Palace of Justice fills a kind of grass platform with its vast, reproving bulk: inside, before an impartial judge gingerly feeling a boil on his neck, my marriage will end without grandeur or glory, after several harrowing months of reconciliations and separations that smashed into anguished smithereens the wreckage of a long, painful winter. We separated amicably enough, well, you probably know how it is, with a feeling that was part relief and part remorse, and we said good-bye in the elevator like two strangers, exchanging a last kiss in which there still lingered an as-yet-undigested remnant of despair. I don't know if this has been your experience too, if you have perhaps known the agony of clandestine weekends in seaside hotels, spent amid the roar of leaden waves crashing against the cracked concrete of the verandah, and where the dunes touch a sky so low and gray that it resembles a shabby stucco ceiling, or if you have embraced a body that you both loved and didn't love in the same anxious haste with which baby monkeys cling to their mother's indifferent fur, or if you have ever, with great conviction, made precipitate promises that sprang more from panic and anxiety than from any genuine and generously tender feelings. For a year, you see, I stumbled from house to house and from woman to woman like a blind child frenziedly groping for an elusive arm, and I often woke up alone in hotels as impersonal as the faces of psychoanalysts, to find myself connected by a numberless phone to the friendly but vaguely suspicious receptionist, who was clearly intrigued by my meager luggage. I ruined teeth and stomach at cheap restaurants that resembled railroad-station buffets, where the food tastes of coal and of sheets damp with the sad mucus of farewells. I went to midnight showings at movie houses, with the lone cougher on the seat behind me sending chills down my neck and reading the subtitles aloud to himself for company. And I discovered, one afternoon, sitting on the seafront at Algés, in the bubbly presence of a bottle of fizzy water, that I was dead, as dead as the suicides who throw themselves off the viaduct and whom we sometimes pass in the street, pale and dignified, a newspaper under one arm, unaware that they are dead, and whose breath smells of meatballs and mashed potatoes and thirty years spent as an exemplary civil servant.

Don't you experience a kind of inner shock when you look into a darkened shopwindow, as if you were gazing into the deviant eye of someone with a divergent squint? When I was small, I often used to imagine, as I lay in bed—my muscles tense with the fear of falling asleep—that everyone had disappeared from the city and I was walking the empty streets pursued by the hollow eyes of statues that watched me with the implacable, inert ferocity of the inanimate, frozen in the artificially pompous pose of photographs from the heroic age, or else avoiding the trees whose leaves trembled with the marine restlessness of fish scales, and even today, you know, I still sometimes imagine myself alone at night in those squares, those petty, melancholy avenues, those side streets like tributaries that drag in their wake suburban haberdashers and decrepit hairdressers, Salão Nelinha, Salão Pereira, Salão Pérola do Faial, with pictures of hairdos cut out of fashion magazines and stuck on the windows. At home, the carpet absorbs the sound of my footsteps, reducing me to the tenuous echo of a shadow, and I have the feeling, when I shave, that once the blade has removed the mentholated foam Santa Claus sideburns from my cheeks, all that will remain of me will be two eyes that hang, suspended, in the mirror, looking around anxiously for their lost body.

Like in Chiúme in December 1971, my first Christmas at war after almost a year in the jungle, a year of despair, expectancy, and death, when I woke in the morning and thought It's Christmas Day today, and then looked outside and saw that nothing had changed in the barracks, the same tents, the same vehicles parked in a circle next to the wire fence, the same abandoned building destroyed by a bazooka, the same slow men stumbling along in the sand or crouched on the crumbling steps of the sergeants' mess, silently scratching the sweat rash in the crooks of their elbows, like beggars on the steps of a church. I woke in the morning to the thunderous sky over the River Cuando and thought It's Christmas Day today, and saw in those same weary gestures the usual eternal Monday morning, the heat was running down my back in large, sticky, sweaty drops, and I said to myself, This can't be right, there's something wrong about all this, my oversize pajamas appeared to contain neither bones nor flesh and I felt that I no longer existed, my trunk, my limbs, my feet didn't exist apart from a pair of blinking eyes staring, in surprise, at the plain and then, beyond the plain, at the accumulation of trees to the north, the direction from which the airplane always came, bringing fresh food and mail, I was just those two astonished, staring eyes, which I rediscover today in the bathroom mirror, looking older and duller after the initial shudder of my first pee, and shouting a silent plea at their own reflection, a plea that goes unanswered.

Days before, a company of parachutists had left, supported by South African helicopters, which had flown in from Cuito-Cuanavale for a pointless, heavy-handed operation in Luchazes, and every night the huge, blond, arrogant pilots would get noisily drunk and smash glasses and bottles and sing out-of-tune Afrikaans songs, led by a rather overweight David Niven lookalike, who watched like an indulgent nanny as his subordinates vomited up beer, leaning on each other for support, green with pain and suffering:

"If you worry, you die. If you don't worry, you die. So, why worry?"

The paratroopers, as strict and grave-faced as lay seminarians, clutching their weapons to their breasts like crucifixes, observed disapprovingly this pandemonium of belches and broken glass, their lips silently mouthing military Our Fathers. The captain, who had the Better Homes and Gardens spirit of a very fastidious house-wife, fluttered anxiously around any crockery still left intact and cast heartrending glances of hopeless passion at the remaining glasses and plates. Second Lieutenant Eleutério sat hunched, fetus-like, in one corner, listening to his Beethoven. The Katangan was sidling off into the village in search of some barbecued rat. Mean-while, I leaned against the window frame watching the ellipses traced by the bats around the lamps, not hearing anything, think-ing anything, wanting anything, convinced that my life would never be more than the wire-fenced oval in which I found myself, beneath a low rainy or misty sky, talking to the chief in the shade of his vast sewing machine, listening to stories about crocodiles in happier times.

The South Africans treated us as if we were some form of accept-able mulatto, and their brute impertinence sparked in me an increasingly rebellious flame, further fanned by the savagery of the PIDE and the abject, patriotic rants on the radio. The politicians in Lisbon seemed to be either criminal puppets or imbeciles defend-ing interests that were not mine and would become less and less mine, and who were simultaneously preparing their own defeat: the men knew very well that the politicians and their sons would never fight and knew where the people rotting in the jungle came from; they had killed and seen far too many people die for them to allow that nightmare to go on for much longer. One night, the rifle-men had marched past the barracks in Luso, shouting insults, and every evening we listened in secret to the MPLA broadcasts; we had to support our wives and children on subsistence wages, and then there were all those cripples hobbling around Lisbon at the end of the day, near the annex to the Military Hospital, and every stump was a cry of revolt against the utter absurdity of bullets. Later, we met with the hostility of Angola's whites, the large landowners and industrialists hidden away in their gigantic mansions replete with fake antiques, from which they would emerge to paw the Brazilian prostitutes in the nightclubs on Luanda Island, where they sat among buckets of appalling local champagne and kisses as loud as the sucking of sink plungers:

"If you lot weren't here, we'd get rid of the blacks in an instant."

Bastards, I thought, as I sat drinking solitary Cuba libres on the balcony, fat, sweaty bastards, fucking fat cats, slave traders, and I envied them those women laughing and whispering into their hairy ears, the plump embraces, the clouds of dense perfume that would emanate from their armpits and groins at the slightest gesture, like smoke from a censer, the inlaid wooden beds in which they would lie down to sleep as morning approached, against a backdrop of dim mirrors, rubber trees in pots, and small Ming dogs, their jaws horribly distorted by ceramic toothache, just as my jaw dropped in incredulity in Chiúme, on that Christmas morning utterly identical to all the other mornings I had known in Africa, staring at the soldiers talking on the other side of the parade ground on the steps of the sergeants' mess, and watching the rain clouds growing over Cuando and heading toward me in great, heavy, basalt billows, threatening a storm.

No, it's not far now, I live over there, in that row of hideous green buildings on which the night confers, by some strange miracle, the profound dignity and rectitude of an abbey, as befits a descendant of storekeepers who, complete with mustache and

watch chain, would stare into the camera lens with bovine distrust, half fear and half respectful superstition. People believed in
God in those days, even as viewed through a tripod camera, a
stern, bearded fellow, a sexagenarian in tunic and sandals and
sporting a middle parting, whose trade in martyrs and saints was
just as complicated an enterprise as the vast emporium of Armazéns
Grandela in downtown Lisbon, involving as it did the distribution
of sins, papal bulls, absolutions, and passports to hell through
earthly intermediaries known as priests, who, each Sunday, sent
the company's director a telex message in Latin. These houses,
don't you think, suit our squat ambitions and our diminutive feelings: the damp gets in, everything warps, the blocked pipes emit
sudden belches and gurgles, the carpets come unglued, the inevi-
table drafts whistle in through the cracks, but we buy furniture in
Sintra to conceal these faults and blotches behind supposedly old-
fashioned frills and flounces, just as we dress up our narrow egotism with the appearance of a vengeful generosity. My father used
to tell me that Philip II had said to the architect of El Escorial, Let
us build something that will make the world say that we were
quite mad. Well, in that case, the order received by the fat, hel-
meted, toothpick-chewing guy who presided over the construction of these monstrous, abstruse, pretentious cages must have
been, Let us build something that will make the world say that we
were mongoloids. And the fact is that the neighbors who squeeze
into the minute elevator with me do have the gaping mouth, dull
eyes, sallow skin, and blithe, uncomprehending smile of creatures
too ordinary ever to be truly unhappy, traversing the desert of the
weekend, seated before their TV sets, sipping the fruit cordial of
their mediocrity through a straw. I, by some miracle, still possess
a residue of metaphysical disquiet and wake in the morning with

sciatica of the soul, cruelly bruised by the footsteps above, and with my intelligence grown rusty after several hours imprisoned in an apartment insidiously designed to transform me into an exhausted functionary carrying a briefcase that contains a copy of *Reader's Digest*, a thermos of coffee for lunch and the jar of royal jelly whose label promises me the illusory eternal youth of an occasional erection.

Anyway, it was Christmas Day in Chiúme and nothing had changed. None of my family was with me, my grandfather's house (with its garden full of statues, the tiled pond, and the greenhouse built onto the dining room) remained painfully anchored in Benfica, behind the brick-red front door and the courtyard full of visitors' cars, the guests, in their Sunday best, would be arriving for lunch, the ancient maids of my childhood would serve bowls of soup, and soon my grandmother would dispatch one of her grandsons to summon the staff so that she could present to them, with all the slow pomp of a Nobel Prize ceremony, soft parcels (containing stockings, underwear, nightdresses, long johns) wrapped in paper dotted with silver stars. Sitting on my bed, looking out at the greenish-yellow vastness of the plain and with the thunderstorm still building over toward Cuando, I remembered my aged aunts' vast apartments in Rua Alexandre Herculano and Rua Barata Salgueiro, which were plunged in an eternal gloom filled by the tinkle of glasses and teapots, Aunt Mimi, Aunt Bilú, an ailing gentleman in an armchair who occasionally ventured some garbled interjection, elderly men, with their hair parted just above one ear and carefully combed over their bald pate, who would distractedly pinch my cheek, I remember the upright pianos, the signed photo of Dom Manuel II, the cookie tins with hunting scenes on the lid. The past, you see, rose up in my memory much as an ill-digested lunch returns in the form of acid reflux: Uncle Elói winding up the wall clocks, the fierce autumn waves at Praia das Maçãs beating against the seawall, the clumsy but suddenly delicate fingers of the caretaker imitating a flower. I had leapt seamlessly from that solemn communion into war, I thought, as I buttoned up my camouflage jacket, they had forced me to confront a death that had nothing in common with the aseptic deaths that occur in hospitals, for the deaths of strangers merely increased my certainty that I was alive and reinforced my agreeable sense of myself as an angelic and eternal being, but, instead, the deaths of my comrades offered me the dizzying sight of my own death in the deaths of those who ate with me, slept with me, talked with me, and occupied the same snug trenches when we were under attack.

A crowd of silhouettes and voices bubbled up in the encampment, came nearer, took shape: my aunts and uncles, my brothers, my cousins, my grandmother's chauffeur, prissy and polite, the men with the comb-overs, the caretaker, the ailing gentleman in the armchair, all in uniform, exhausted, dirty, guns at their shoulders, were returning from an operation in the jungle and heading for the infirmary, carrying on an improvised stretcher my dislocated, inert body, with a tourniquet around what had been my thigh, which was now nothing but a bloody, swollen mess. I recognized myself as if in an all-too-truthful mirror as I examined my closed eyes, my pale mouth, the fair growth of beard darkening my chin, the pale mark left by my lost wedding ring on my now-ringless hand. Someone was cutting up the Christmas cake with ritual gestures, my wife, moved to tears, was waiting with a plastic grocery bag full of presents for me. The family standing motionless at the door to the first-aid post were waiting, in suspense, for me to bring myself back to life, the radio officer was screaming down the line for a helicopter to take me to Benfica in time for the liqueurs and coffee. I listened to my heart and no sound reached my ears through the rubber tubes of the stethoscope. The medic handed me a syringe full of adrenaline, and then I unbuttoned my shirt, felt for the space between my ribs, and stuck the needle straight into my heart.

P

———————

*H*ere we are. No, I haven't had too much to drink, I often try the wrong key first, perhaps because I find it hard to accept that this building is mine and that the balcony up there, in darkness, belongs to the apartment where I live. I feel, you see, like one of those dogs that sniffs away, intrigued, at the smell of his own urine on the tree he's just left behind, and I stand here for a few minutes, surprised and incredulous, caught between the mailboxes and the elevator, searching in vain for some mark of my own, a footprint, a smell, an article of clothing, an object, in the empty atmosphere of the hall, whose silent, neutral nakedness always throws me somehow. If I open my mailbox, I never find a letter, a circular, even a piece of paper bearing my name to prove that I exist, that I live here, that, in a way, this place belongs to me. You have no idea how I envy the tranquil certainty of my neighbors, the familiar decisiveness with which they open the door, the proprietorial disdain with which they examine the newspaper headlines as they wait for the elevator, the knowing friendliness of their smiles: there lingers in me the stubborn suspicion that they'll throw me out one day, that when I go into my apartment, I'll find someone else's furniture in there, strange books on the shelves, a child's voice somewhere down the corridor, a man sitting on my sofa and looking up at me, indignant and perplexed. One night, not long ago, when I answered the phone, the voice at the other end asked for a completely different number from mine. Did I disabuse them or hang up? No, I realized I was trembling, the words got stuck in my throat, I was damp with sweat and embarrassment, I sat perched on the edge of the chair in an excess of guilty politeness, feeling that I was a stranger in a strange apartment, fraudulently invading another person's privacy, the thief of another person's domestic universe. As her children left home one by one, my mother transformed all our bedrooms into living rooms, the beds disappeared, unfamiliar pictures appeared on the walls, and our presence was erased from the rooms we had once inhabited, much as one hurries to wash one's hands after shaking a particularly unpleasant greasy palm. Later, when we would go back there for family suppers, the house was at once familiar and foreign: we recognized the smells, the chests of drawers, the faces, but instead of ourselves, we found childhood photos of us scattered about the tables, smiling with the broad, disquieting innocence of the very young, and it seemed to me that the photograph of me as a boy had devoured the adult I had become, and that the person who really existed there was a lock of fair hair above a striped smock looking accusingly at me through the diffuse mist of years separating us. We never are where we are, wouldn't you agree, not even now, squashed together in this cramped elevator, you stiff and silent, gauging out of the corner of your eye my goatish intentions, I jingling my keys with the nervous impatience I invariably feel when I enter one of these strange contraptions for traveling up and down, modern-day substitutes for hot-air balloons and always on the verge of plummeting helplessly, catastrophically earthward. You, for example, are sunbathing nude on the beach last August before the syrupy, domesticated Algarve sea, accompanied by one of those plain but intelligent women whom it's easy enough to like because, on the one hand, they represent no competition and, on the other, they save you from having to go alone to movies at the Gulbenkian Center, a place largely frequented by lucid myopes and peremptory sociologists, and I am still in Angola as I was eight years ago, saying good-bye to the chief-cum-tailor and his prehistoric sewing machine, covered now by a thick moss of rust, which the sand corrodes and tortures much as Giacometti, in a kind of patient rage, used to sculpt his painful, long-legged silhouettes, like imaginary birds that are more real than the real thing. We're about to leave Chiúme and head north, the vehicles are waiting in line for us to climb aboard, and I am standing motionless in the middle of the encampment, sickened by the putrid smell of manioc drying like white bones on the hut roofs, I am trying desperately, on this January morning washed by the night rain and bathed in an excess of light that dissolves the edges of things and drowns in its pitiless brilliance any delicate or overly fragile feelings, I'm trying, as I said, to fix in my mind the scene I've inhabited for so many months, the canvas tents, the stray dogs, the decrepit buildings of the defunct administration that is gradually dying in a slow agony of neglect: the idea of a Portuguese Africa, which the history books at school, the politicians' speeches, and the chaplain in Mafra all described in such majestic terms, was, after all, a kind of provincial backwater rotting away in the vastness of space, a sort of housing project rapidly devoured by grass and scrub, a great, desolate silence inhabited by the gnarled and starving figures of the lepers. This land at the end of the world was extremely isolated and extremely poor, governed by drunken, greedy district leaders, trembling with malaria in their empty houses, reigning over a people resigned to their fate who sat at the doors of their huts with a kind of vegetable indifference. Admiral Tomás glared down at us from the wall with the foolish, glassy stare of a stuffed bear, militiamen carrying venerable shotguns dozed in their own shadow beneath the corrugated iron roofs of the sentry boxes next to the futile wire fence. Meanwhile, there was the almost ethereal beauty of the eucalyptus trees of Ninda or Cessa, imprisoning in their branches a dense, neverending night, the angry majesty of the jungle of Chalala resisting the bombs, the tattooed pubises of the women, behind whose teapot curve of belly grew, to the cardiac beat of drums, children whom I desperately hoped would be less passive and less melancholic, who would not crouch submissively outside their huts, passing around a pipe.

No, it's here, sixth floor, on the left, a marble hallway, would you believe, a different-colored carpet in every room and a TV socket too, five rooms, three bathrooms, two long balconies overlooking the cemetery, the Tagus, and the orange sun at the end of the day swallowed up by the rooftops of Areeiro. I feel like a displaced ostrich here and wander from room to room talking to myself, the way old people do, a glass of whisky in my hand, reciting to the ice cubes the black-and-white sonnets of Antero de Quental that populated my childhood with cosmic ghosts. The landlord, a guy with a very affirmative mustache, visits me now and then in a fancy American car whose extraordinary profusion of headlights, embellishments, and chrome always makes me think of an ornate Manueline church fitted with radial tires, anyway, he equipped the three identical bathrooms with baptismal fonts that oblige me to brush my teeth in the morning murmuring prayers in Latin, he replaced the wardrobe doors with wood panels that lack only the hesitant smiles of a gallery of medieval saints to be complete, and he offered me the extra gift of a garage-cum-catacomb in the depths of the building, where my modest cough reverberates with the tragic echo of an avalanche. Gradually, I began to get used to this Chartres Cathedral made for prosaic customs officers whose nightmares bristle with invoices and balance sheets, and I began to love the horrible colors of the walls and the absence of furniture, just as one can grow to love a hunchbacked child or a woman with bad breath, out of boredom, out of habit, or even, perhaps, as a way of expiating obscure sins. I like the baptismal fonts, the wardrobes, the view of the cemetery of Alto de São João that I can see from the kitchen and that seems to be a remarkable blend of Portugal dos Pequenitos* and the dog cemetery at the zoo, part of the nitrogen cycle. And luckily I can't see the sea from here, so there's no danger of my eyes gazing out at the horizon in search of drifting islands or the troubling caravels of some inner adventure, always ready to set sail for an imaginary India. No, you can't see the sea, only a rather banal strip of river cut short by a mist of concrete factories and the roofs, roofs, roofs and façades that shelter our contented contemporaries, patiently collecting the butterflies or stamps of their unambitious boredom, or else mentally taking the bread knife to their wives seated in the armchair next to them, knitting. I'm sure that if I were to lock myself in and stay here for a whole month, sitting at my desk, without talking to anyone, without answering the door or the phone, without responding to the entreaties of the cleaning woman, the concierge, or the man from the gas company who occasionally

---

* Portugal dos Pequenitos (Little Portugal) is a theme park that includes miniature versions of Portugal's most famous monuments and examples of domestic architecture.

comes to read the gas meter, if I were to spend that month, brows knitted, scribbling stern notes to myself, I would gradually metamorphose into the perfect insect of a colonel in the army reserves or a retiree from a savings and loan, corresponding in Esperanto with a Persian bank clerk or a Swedish watchmaker, and drinking lime tea on the balcony after supper, checking the unshaven faces of my collection of cacti.

No, seriously, happiness, that vague state resulting from an impossible convergence of parallel lines in the form of a good digestion and a smug egotism untouched by regrets, still seems to me—for I belong to the glum category of the sad and restless, eternally waiting for an explosion or a miracle—something as abstract and strange as innocence, justice, honor, those profound, grandiloquent, and ultimately empty concepts that the family, school, the catechism, and the State solemnly imposed upon me so as to tame me more easily, to nip in the bud, if I may put it like that, any stirrings of protest and rebellion. What others demand of us, you understand, is that we don't cause them to doubt, that we don't disturb their teeny-tiny lives, which they have carefully insulated against despair and hope, that we don't shatter their aquariums of deaf fish floating in the slimy water of the day-to-day, lit obliquely by the sleepy lamp of what we call virtue, which, when looked at closely, turns out to be merely the lukewarm absence of ambition.

Would you like a whisky? Nowadays, this banal yellow liquid constitutes, apart from the circumnavigation of the world and the arrival of the first diving suit on the moon, our one chance of adventure: by the fifth glass, the floor imperceptibly takes on the rather pleasing slant of a ship's deck, by the eighth, the future assumes the victorious dimensions of Austerlitz, by the tenth, we are sliding slowly into a viscous coma, stammering out the clumsy syllables of happiness. So, if you don't mind, I'll sit down beside you on the sofa to have a better view of the river and to drink to the future and that coma.

Eastern Angola? I'm still there in a way, sitting next to the driver in one of the trucks in the column, bumping along the sandy tracks to Malanje. Ninda, Luate, Lusse, Nengo, rivers swollen with rain flowing under wooden bridges, leper colonies, the red earth of Gago Coutinho that sticks to your skin and your hair, the eternally anxious lieutenant colonel nervously shrugging his shoulders as he sits before a glass of crème de cacao, the PIDE agents in Mete Lenha's café, shooting dull, hate-filled glances at the blacks sipping timid, fearful beers at the next tables. No one who comes here is ever the same again, I was saying to the captain, he of the wire-rimmed spectacles and the membranous fingers moving the chess pieces on the board as delicately as a goldsmith, even we survivors have several legs missing, several arms missing, several feet of intestine missing; when we amputated the gangrenous leg of the MPLA guerrilla we captured in Mussuma, the soldiers had their photo taken with it as if it were a trophy, the war has made animals of us, you see, cruel, stupid animals trained to kill, there wasn't an inch of wall in the barracks unadorned by a picture of a naked woman, we masturbated and ejaculated, this is the world-created-by-the-Portuguese, these blacks hollow with hunger who don't understand our language, it's sleeping sickness, malaria, amebiasis, poverty, when we reached Luso, a Jeep drove up to inform us that the general wouldn't let us sleep in town or show our all-too-evident scars in the mess. We're not mad dogs, yelled the half-crazy lieutenant to the messenger, tell that stupid prick we're not mad dogs, a second lieutenant muttered something about blowing up the mess with bazookas. Let's screw 'em all, sir, then there won't be a single one of the bastards left to get on our tits, A year in the back of beyond doesn't necessarily give us the right to a night in a proper bed, said the officer in charge of operations very sensibly, the lieutenant thumped the hood of the Jeep hard, Tell our general to piss off, We weren't mad dogs when we arrived here, I said to the lieutenant, who was seething with anger and indignation, we weren't mad dogs before the censored letters, the attacks, the ambushes, the mines, the lack of food and tobacco and cold drinks and matches and water and coffins, before we were told that a Berliet truck was worth more than a man and before we found out that the death of a soldier merited just three lines in the newspaper, He died in combat in Angola, we weren't mad dogs, it's simply that we meant nothing to the mealy-mouthed State, who shat on us and used us as laboratory rats and who now at least are afraid of us, so afraid of our presence, of our unpredictable reactions and the remorse we represent that they cross the road if they see us coming, they avoid us, they don't want to face a battalion destroyed in the name of a lot of cynical ideas no one believes in, a battalion destroyed merely to defend the wealth of the three or four families who shore up the regime, the giant lieutenant turned to me, touched my arm and begged in a voice that was suddenly a child's voice, Doctor, fix me up with some illness before I explode right here in the street from all the shit inside me.

Q

------

*Y*ou find the apartment a little bare, do you? You're right, it lacks paintings, books, knickknacks, chairs, a judicious scattering of magazines and papers, of clothes thrown down on the bed, of ash on the floor, in short, it lacks all those things that assure us we still exist, can still move, breathe, eat, get excited about the indifferent seasons and the distracted silhouette of the man in the Sandeman advertisement, who, flashing on and off above the rooftops overlooking the Rossio,* proposes us a derisive toast. This stiff, empty tomb where I live also gives me a sense that it's all provisional, ephemeral, a mere interval, and that, I must say, delights me: I can still consider myself to be a man, but not just yet, and thus postpone the present indefinitely until I rot without ever having ripened, my eyes still glinting with youth and mischief like those of some old village woman. I can lie in bed and watch through my curtainless windows the men on the construction site opposite, who start work far earlier than I do and regard me from the other side of the street

------

* The Rossio is the familiar name for the Praça de Dom Pedro IV, a large square in the center of Lisbon.

with a kind of astonished envy. Sleepy-eyed women lean from balconies and shake out their energetic, exhausted dust cloths. Tiny tugboats with bad backs pull fat, placid ships toward the harbor bar. Even in the cemetery, there's probably a lot of noisy morning activity among family skeletons, a mutual, meticulous picking off of worms, like mandrills picking at lice. Meanwhile I, the sole inhabitant of this deserted apartment, generously allow myself the languid pleasures of idleness because I will only emerge from my hibernation at night when I go to the bar where we met, under those Art Nouveau lamps and those hunting scenes, my nose buried in the vodka-and-orange that constitutes my very late breakfast.

Life lived against the current does, however, have its disadvantages: my friends gradually distanced themselves from me, annoyed by what they considered to be an emotional frivolity bordering on dissolute vagrancy. My family recoiled from my kisses as if from a bad case of contagious acne. My professional colleagues gleefully put out the word that I was a dangerous incompetent, having first, of course, referred briefly to a brilliant future ruined by Mafia-style orgies at which I would sit with a feather-adorned French dancer from the Estoril Casino on each devilish knee. Even my patients became suspicious of the dark shadows under my eyes and of my equivocal breath on which there still lingered an evident whiff of alcohol. I made the nights ever longer and the days ever shorter in the hope that a perpetual night would throw a modest veil of shadow over my greenish complexion: this absurd city—in which the glazed tiles multiply and reflect back the smallest scrap of brightness in an endless game of mirrors, and where objects drift, suspended, in the light as they do in paintings by Matisse—this city forced me to stumble from room to room like a bewildered butterfly, stroking the repellent rasp of my beard with one soft palm.

Yes, the apartment is a little bare, but have you considered how much space this leaves for dreams, not domestic, conjugal dreams of furniture that require one to count the pennies needed to buy a writing desk or a chest of drawers, but dreams *tout court*, with no clear goals or defined objectives, whose tonality varies and whose shape changes ceaselessly, a dream *à la* Infante Dom Henrique* made up of unknown seas, monsters, and spices, the caravel that one sends off down the carpet in the corridor and whose problematic return one awaits in the marble hallway, consulting the curious astrolabe of a comic strip. This apartment, my friend, is the Gobi Desert, miles and miles of sand with no oasis, and in which my mute mouth closes over yellow camel teeth. So when someone invades my solitude, I feel, you understand, like a hermit meeting another hermit on the edge of a plague of locusts, and I try painfully to recall the Morse code of words, relearning the sounds like an aphasic having to start all over, with great difficulty, to use a code he has forgotten.

Another whisky? It's best we forearm ourselves against this night that is liable, with no advance warning, to grow light and give way to a horribly clear, bright morning, in which our blurred silhouettes, made for the indulgent complicity of the shadows, will dissolve like perfume from old bottles, from which emanates the sweet smell of dead passions, we should wall ourselves in with alcohol to defend ourselves from the all-revealing sun that holds up to our eyes, with the implacable cruelty of a mirror, faces crumpled from lack of sleep, dull eyes blinking beneath a shock of disastrously

* The Infante Dom Henrique (1394–1460), better known in English as Henry the Navigator, a prince of Portugal, was responsible for sponsoring Portuguese voyages of discovery to Madeira and the west coast of Africa.

disheveled hair. It sometimes happens that I wake up next to a woman I met in a bar only a few hours before, beneath the light of some propitious lamp, whose opaline glow lent wrinkles and crow's-feet the insidious charm of a judicious maturity, alas, the raising of the blind reveals, all too brutally, a vulnerable creature prematurely aged, shipwrecked among the sheets in a state of abandon whose very fragility enrages me. Sitting on the bed, resting my head on the pillow I've propped against the wall, I light the cigarette of disillusion and anger, staring sourly at the bracelets and rings placed in a neat pile on the bedside table, at the unfamiliar clothes on the floor, the black bra draped over a chair like a bat waiting for darkness to come in order to leave its rafter in the attic. Her mouth occasionally burbles words that have slipped surreptitiously out of dreams to which I have no access, the soft curve of her shoulder shudders with indecipherable fears, the hair between her open legs has lost the mysterious look of a dense forest, which, earlier on, received me into its soft vegetable hollow. The anger of deceit swells my testicles and my cock, a feeling impossible to master or control or diminish, and I end up penetrating her, dizzy with loathing, like someone sticking a knife in someone's belly in a brawl in a bar, only to hear later on, my teeth gritted, her grateful poodle whimperings in response to what she imagines to be an enthusiastic homage to the quality of her charms.

A double, no ice? You're right, perhaps that way you'll achieve the illusionless lucidity of Hemingway's drunks, who, with each drink they took, gradually moved beyond anxiety, reaching a kind of polar serenity, a close cousin of death, it's true, but it is made almost soothing and joyful by the absence of hope and frantic yearning that inevitably accompanies it, and maybe then you'll be able to confront the ferocity of morning from inside a protective bottle of Logan's, just as the corpses of animals are preserved in special liquids on the shelves of museums. Perhaps that way you'll be able to smile like Socrates after drinking the hemlock, get out of bed, go over to the window, and, faced by the bright, busy, noisy, matutinal city, not feel pursued by the pitiless ghosts of your own solitude, whose sad, sardonic faces, so similar to our own, etch themselves on the glass the better to mock us: as you see, some defeats can be transformed into victorious calamities.

In the North, for want of whisky, we used to drink the evil, sulfurous brews provided by the administrator, a big, fat Indian who received the officers with the amiable pomp of an absolute monarch, in order to have the pleasure of hearing his own voice in the ears of others, whose distracted attention proved to him the existence of an audience, just as our faces in the mirror, when we're shaving, guarantee us the certainty of the face we were beginning to doubt, like stumbling angels who hesitate when confronted by the opacity of the flesh. The company passed briefly through Malanje, where the battalion took up temporary residence in the uncomfortable shell of the barracks, then, abandoning the night of the city, dark and opaque as the eyes of a gypsy, headed for Baixa do Cassanje, endless fields of sunflowers and cotton against a background of unreal beauty, and the poverty of the villages by the roadside, where ancient black men crouched like coarse bread rolls on smooth, dark rocks. We stopped in Marimba, a long line of enormous mango trees at the top of a hill surrounded by the distant blue of the fields, in a new circle of wire on which the local kids from the neighboring villages hung their starving faces, while fat rain clouds, as heavy as udders, gathered over the River Cambo, inhabited by the mineral silence of crocodiles.

There, for a year, we did not die the death of war, which empties your head with one huge blast and leaves around you a disjointed desert of moans and a confusion of panic and shots, but the slow, painful, tormenting agony of waiting, waiting for the months to pass, waiting for the mines along the jungle paths, waiting for malaria, waiting for the ever-more-improbable return home, with family and friends at the airport or on the dock, waiting for letters, waiting for the PIDE Jeep that passed each week on its way to meet informers on the frontier, bringing with it three or four prisoners who dug their own graves, then hunched down inside them, closed their eyes tight, and, when the bullet was fired, crumpled the way a soufflé collapses, a red flower of blood opening its petals on their heads.

"A one-way ticket to Luanda," said the PIDE agent, calmly tucking his pistol under his arm. "You can't trust these bastards an inch."

And so, when the same guy cut his bottom on the broken toilet seat, I sewed up his wound without anesthetic, in the cubicle in the first-aid post, beneath the contented gaze of the nurse, thus wreaking a small revenge, with each howl of pain he uttered, on behalf of those silent men who dug their own graves, panic spreading in great sheets of sweat on their skinny backs, and who fixed us with eyes as hard and inscrutable as stones, empty of light, just like the naked dead stretched out in the hospital's mortuary icebox.

After supper, the reluctant electricity generator caused a constellation of stuttering lamps to spark into life and these, in turn, partially lit the row of mango trees, plucking a few tragic branches from the darkness, and we officers made a formal visit to the administrator's house for a game of lotto, at which Dona Áurea, the wife of the local emperor, glittering with earrings and necklaces, her ample, aging bosom almost bursting out of her low-cut dress, would distribute the cards and the chickpeas we used as counters, and from a bag that looked identical to the shrouds that, in my childhood, were thrown over the sewing machine that was kept in a narrow room full of laundry baskets and the fresh smell of washed sheets, she would draw out the wooden numbers and announce them in a low, intimate, confiding voice. At the other end of the room, her husband, bowing gallantly, would invite the primary-school teacher to dance to the record player's slow, slurred tangos. She was a very thin woman, with collarbones as prominent as Brezhnev's eyebrows, and suffered from interminable periods that afflicted her with colic and anemia; she would fix us with exhausted, darkly shadowed eyes that spoke of fainting fits and arithmetic. Gilt-framed watercolors of hyacinths and dahlias hung, fading, on the walls. The thunder over the River Cambo lit the window with what looked like the pretend lightning flashes you get in theatres in Portugal, when one suspects the presence, behind a curtain, of some fellow laboriously flicking switches on and off. The mulatto, owner of the only shop in town, would doze, toothpick in mouth, snoring peacefully, like a hippopotamus in a coma. The local bus driver adjusted his forelock with the kind of plastic yellow comb tourists buy at the seaside. The evening passed in a languor of occasional coughs and weary pleasantries, until Dona Áurea turned to the door, raised her head like a coyote about to howl, filled her flaccid chest with a breath worthy of a deep-sea diver, and gave a long, imperious roar:

"Bonifáciooooooooo!"

A few seconds of expectant silence followed while the mulatto, rudely awakened, looked around wildly, asking:

"What's wrong? What's wrong?"

as if he were on a raft careering off course. Shortly afterward, we would hear the hasty tinkle of glasses in the kitchen, and a Chaplinesque black fellow squeezed into a tight, *Gone-With-the-Wind*–style butler's jacket, would come dancing down the corridor in his vast shoes, carrying a tray full of bottles that one expected, at any moment, to crash to the floor in a shower of silent-movie slivers. The whisky tasted of lamp oil and cheap soap, and we all sacrificially drank a couple of fingers of that jaundice-yellow liquid, grimacing behind our hands, while the administrator, putting the chickpeas from the game of lotto back in the numbers bag, exclaimed:

"Good stuff, eh?"

and received from the captain an obedient, resigned, cod-liver-oil smile.

Outside, the *cipaio* guarding the electricity generator, and armed with the kind of musket used by the Spanish conquistadors, was snoring under the concrete roof. Bats the size of partridges swooped and dived around the lamps, pale fires burned out in the dense night of the villages—of Chief Macau, Chief Pedro Macau, Chief Marimba—that had been built beside the runway, which was under constant invasion by scrub, and, in the distance, the lights of Chiquita trembled brightly, like a constellation of improbable stars. Immediately after the war started, they had killed, or driven over the border into Congo, the Mo-holos and Bundi-Bangalas who originally lived in Baixa do Cassanje, and had filled their villages with Jingas from around Luanda, who were more obedient and accommodating because their chief had spent twenty years rotting in colonial prisons on the pretext of some crime or other. Wearing a tin crown encrusted with glass diamonds and made to look ridiculous in the eyes of his own people by the State, which forced him to wear the humiliating uniform of a Carnival emperor, the chief wandered about his village much as the mentally ill do in psychiatric wards and was accordingly eyed with incredulous disgust by the old men of the tribe. Meanwhile, Chief Bimbe and Chief Caputo, on the other side of the frontier, continued the struggle, and from Marimbanguengo you could see the MPLA bases in the Congo, minuscule constructions that were nonetheless growing. Dona Áurea bowed in friendly fashion to the teacher, she of the Niagaran periods, who was furtively scratching the sweat rash in her armpits.

"And how is your health, Dona Olinda?"

You cannot imagine (just a drop, thank you, that's perfect, stop) the strangeness of that game of lotto in the middle of the jungle, of those fusty old tangos cranked out on a record player, of the women's pathetically elaborate getups, the men bowing, the watercolor dahlias on the wall, while those condemned by PIDE lay coiled like lifeless tentacles in their holes, and the soldiers shook with malarial fever in their bunks in the barracks, the generals in air-conditioned Luanda invented a war in which we would die and they would live, the African night unfolded in a majestic infinity of stars, the workers bought in Nova Lisboa died of homesickness in the estate villages, and I wrote to my folks back home, Everything's fine here, in the hope that they would understand from my tender, nostalgic words the cruel futility of all that suffering, sadism, and separation, that they would understand from what I said what I couldn't say, which was the Fuck fuck fuck fuck fuck fuck of the medic after the ambush, if you remember, in the East, in that land of empty sand occupied by the Luchazi, with the corporal's dead body rotting beneath the blanket in my room, and me sitting on the steps of the first-aid post just as I'm sitting here with you in this room, watching the boats on the river in our reflection in the glass, with me talking and you listening with a sarcastic attention that troubles and confuses me. Women, said Voltaire, are incapable of irony, fourteen very careful stitches in the PIDE agent's ass, drawing the needle through his flesh with delicious slowness, let me rest my head on your knees for a moment and close my eyes, the same eyes that watched the *cipaio* shoving ice cubes up some guy's ass and me not uttering a word of protest, out of fear, you understand, fear froze the slightest gesture of revolt, my selfish self wanted to go home unscathed and soon, before an impeding prison door closed on me, to go home and forget and resume my hospital work and my writing and my family and the cinema on Saturdays and my friends as if nothing had happened to me in the meantime, to disembark in Rocha do Conde de Óbidos and say to myself, It was all a lie, and yet I wake up on nights like this, when the alcohol emphasizes my feelings of abandonment and loneliness, and, finding myself at the bottom of an inner well that is too deep, too narrow, too smooth, there rises up in me, as clearly as when it happened eight years ago, the memory of my cowardice and my egotism, a memory I thought had been locked away forever in some lost drawer in my mind, and a kind of, how can I put it, a kind of remorse that makes me curl up in one corner of my room like a hunted animal, white with shame and fear, waiting, my mouth resting on my knees, for a morning that never comes.

R

No, it never comes, the morning never comes, it's pointless waiting for the rooftops to grow pale, for an icy pallor to shed a tremulous light on the blinds, for small groups of numb creatures, brutally torn from the womb of sleep, to gather at bus stops on their way to a job that gives them no pleasure: we are condemned, you and I, to a thick, dense, despairing, endless night, with no refuge and no way out, a labyrinth of anguish on which the whisky casts an oblique, turbid glow, as we sit side by side on the sofa, clutching our empty glasses like pilgrims to Fátima clutching their extinguished candles, emptied of words, feelings, life, smiling at each other like china dogs on a living-room shelf, our eyes exhausted from week after terrified week of keeping watch. Have you noticed how the silence of four o'clock in the morning instills in one the same kind of disquiet that inhabits the trees before the wind comes, a leafy tremor of the hair, a trunklike trembling of the intestines, a shaking of the roots of our feet that we cross and uncross for no reason? We're basically waiting for what will not happen, the longing that makes our pulses race is pedaling away inside us like those fixed bicycles you get in gyms, because tonight, you see, is a basement set adrift, a vast wardrobe to which we've lost the key, a fishless aquarium shipwrecked on an absence of rocks, and it can only be crossed in the dark on the waters of a formless disquiet. We will stay where we are, listening to the refrigerator motor, the only living company in the gloom, the icebox's white light making the tiles glow phosphorescent like the wall of an igloo, until they build other buildings on top of this one, other streets on top of this street, until faces of cool indifference replace the brief friendliness of my current neighbors, until the concierge acquires the magnificent, gauzy beard of a village idiot, and the archaeologists of the future find our bodies frozen in a posture of waiting, just like the chalk figures on Etruscan tombs, waiting, with a glass of whisky in one hand, for the brightness of an atomic dawn.

Meanwhile, if you agree, we could perhaps try making love, or rather that form of pagan gymnastics that, once the exercise is over, leaves on the body and on the disaster area of the sheets a taste of sweat and sadness: my bed doesn't creak, and it's unlikely that my upstairs neighbor's toilet will, at this hour, vomit up the slimy contents of its stomach, disturbing the affectless caresses that are like the start-up motor of desire, well, neither of us feels for the other more than the solidarity felt by tubercular patients in a sanatorium, the melancholy sadness of a shared fate: we have lived long enough not to run the foolish risk of falling in love, of feeling in our guts and in our souls the excitement of an adventure, of spending whole afternoons on the other side of the street, staring at a closed door, holding a bunch of flowers, swallowing anxiously, as ridiculous and touching as that Eça de Queiroz character, José Matias.* Time has

---

*Eça de Queiroz (1845–1900), Portugal's greatest nineteenth-century novelist, author of *The Crime of Father Amaro* and *The Maias*.

given us the wisdom of skepticism and cynicism, we lost the frank simplicity of youth with our second suicide attempt, when we awoke in the hospital beneath the celestial gaze of a St. Peter wearing a stethoscope, and we distrust humanity as much as we distrust ourselves, because we know that behind the deceptive varnish of generosity lies a sour egotism. It's not that I don't trust you, it's me I don't trust, my aversion to giving myself to anyone, my panic at feeling loved, my inexplicable need to destroy the fleeting, day-to-day moments of pleasure, crushing them with my acid comments and my irony and reducing them to the usual bitter, boring mush. What would become of us if we were actually happy? Have you ever thought how perplexed and confused we would be, looking anxiously about us in search of some comforting misfortune, the way children look around for the smiling face of some family member at a school party? Have you noticed how frightened we are if someone, completely genuinely, with no ulterior motives, gives themselves to us, how unbearable we find that kind of sincere, unconditional love that asks nothing in return? We hasten to kill the Camilo Torreses, Che Guevaras, and Allendes* of this world because their combative love makes us feel uncomfortable, we angrily seek them out in the jungles of Bolivia with a bazooka on our shoulder, we bomb their palaces, we replace them with cruel, slimy creatures, more like us, whose mustaches don't make us vomit with remorse. And so sexual relations between you and me would be a kind of flabby violation, a hasty exhibition of joyless loathing, the damp defeat of two exhausted bodies on the mattress, each of us waiting to get our breath back

* Salvador Allende (1908–1973) was the democratically elected president of Chile from 1970–1973. He died during the military coup led by Augusto Pinochet, when the presidential palace was attacked from the air and the ground.

before glancing at our watches on the bedside table, getting dressed in silence, quickly checking makeup and hair in the bathroom mirror, then leaving, under cover of darkness, our skin still moist from the other person, and going back to the solitude of our own apartments. Those who live together and reluctantly share the same duvet and toothpaste suffer a similar sense of isolation: ah, the meals eaten in silence opposite one another, full of a rancor you can smell in the air like a widow's cologne! The evenings spent watching TV and plotting vengeful conjugal murders, the fish knife, the Chinese jar, a timely shove out of the window! The minutely detailed dreams of your husband having a heart attack or your wife a thrombosis, the pain in the chest, the mouth askew, the childish words dribbled out onto the hospital pillow! We at least have the advantage of being able to sleep alone, without someone else's leg exploring the cooler areas of the sheet that, by geographical right, belong to us, but, at the same time, we lack someone to blame for our deep dissatisfaction with ourselves, an easy target for our insults, a victim, in short, for our own spiteful mediocrity. You and I, thank God, don't run that risk, we are like two judo experts who fear each other enough not to hurt each other and, at most, invent false, inoffensive blows that stop halfway, like tentacles that reach out and then withdraw: if I were to tell you that I love you, you would reply, in the most serious tones you could muster, that you haven't liked a man as much since you were eighteen, that you feel something different, strange, and troubling, that you want more than anything else in the world never to be parted from me, and we would end up laughing into our respective whisky glasses at the innocuous innocence of our lies. But what if, for a few moments, we were to take off the bulletproof vest of world-weary guile and were, for example, to be sincere with each other? What if, when I stroked your hand, I was touching not just your fingers as they are now, beginning to age beneath your rings, but the narrow wrist of a fragile, vulnerable girl chewing gum in the shadow of the scornful, tragic photo of that blond archangel, James Dean, whose brief, cometlike flight ended abruptly in a smoking pile of scrap metal? What if your nipples were to grow hard with real desire, a strange shiver drive your thighs apart, and your belly contract with an intense, inexplicable desire for me? What a drag, eh? Jealousy, exclusivity, the dreadful torment of feeling the other person's absence. Don't worry, it's too late for that, it will always be too late for us, an excess of lucidity keeps us safe from the stupid, ardent impulses of passion, my thinning hair and your crow's-feet, impossible to disguise beneath your polite smile, protect us from the enthusiasm of being alive, from tender dreams, from the pure, untarnished contentment of believing in other people.

We are, therefore, in a condition to go over to that bed and make love, a love as insipid as that frozen fish we ate in the restaurant, whose one eye fixed us with the dying glassy glare of an octogenarian among the faded green of the lettuce. Your mouth has the taste-free taste of old cookies wrapped in the sugar of your lipstick, my tongue is a piece of sponge curled around your teeth and swollen with the oily foam of our mingled saliva. We will come together like two great Tertiary-age monsters, bristling with cartilage and bones, bleating out the onomatopoeic groans of vast lizards, while outside, the jungle paths of the north, washed away by the rains, replace the black-glass ribbon of the river, bubbling with lights, and I jump up beside the driver of the Unimog truck on our way to Dala-Samba, protected by an escort of men lurching around in the back on a wooden bench, and I sit there, swaying, with a box full of cholera vaccine rattling around on my lap.

Now and then, when I felt I was almost moldering away from

inertia in that barbed-wire compound—watching the bats in the mango trees, playing lotto at the administrator's house, studying how the mineral-eyed geckos on the ceiling swallowed the instantaneous Communion wafers of moths—when I felt crushed by the sheer monotony and my own feelings of impatience, when the officers' card game seemed to me an absurd ritual gradually taking on the sinister characteristics of a blood ritual (Eight or nothing, you fucker), when, after masturbating, I would lie awake, unable to sleep, staring out of the window at the thunder over Cambo and thinking about your thighs in Lisbon, the slight swish of your stockings as you crossed your legs, the triangular fuzz of hair through which I ran my fingers, the taste of oysters hidden away in the lace of your panties, when the dogs whining outside the kitchen sounded almost human, like hungry children, when my daughter started to walk with the hesitant, conscientious steps of a mechanical toy, holding on to the chairs as she did so, when time stagnated in the deep well of the calendars as stubbornly as a stone with roots, and the endless afternoon naps lasted months and months, I would set off for Dala-Samba, next to Baixa do Cassanje, to visit the cemeteries of the Jinga kings perched on top of bare hills and surrounded by clusters of palm trees bent low by the wind of death. Zé do Telhado's grave* was in Dala, close to the two or three dusty stores in that abandoned settlement, where the old, almost poverty-stricken farmers grew green with malaria, a few goats sported sculptor's goatees in the silence surrounding the huts, and the male nurse in Caombo Hospital in his immaculate gown spoke the beautiful Por-

---

*Zé do Telhado (1818–1875) was a famous highwayman in Portugal, the Portuguese equivalent of Robin Hood. In 1861, he was condemned to exile in Angola, where he became a trader in rubber and ivory.

tuguese of a countess. We slept in the white iron beds of the maternity ward, among cupboards full of surgical instruments and gynecological tables, and when we woke, the previous night's storm had washed the morning clean, polishing its surfaces and buffing its colors, and when we went out to the trucks, I felt as if I were stepping into the first day of creation, before the parting of the waters, as if I were floating, swaying about in my soldier's boots, in the unreal clarity of old photographs, where the iodine bleaches the shapes of people and the expressions on their faces into one dazzling sunspot.

If you had known the African dawns in Baixa do Cassanje, the vigorous smell of the earth and the grass, the blurred silhouettes of the trees, the pure-white shroud of the cotton fields stretching as far as the horizon, perhaps then it would be possible for us to go back to the beginning, to the as-yet-timid answers exchanged over our first whisky, to the smile that asks and the sideways glance that consents, and build on that the seamless complicity of lovers, who, at a stroke, slay all distrust and fear and snore in unison in guesthouses, sated and satisfied. To judge by all those necklaces, though, the chalky dust of Morocco is the nearest you've ever been to the equator, and your foretaste of paradise was, therefore, a few old men crouched outside grubby houses, a kind of Algarve invaded by gypsies spouting some nauseating, incomprehensible spiel and trying to sell you rugs and cheap bracelets. Far from the Manueline filigree of the Monastery of the Jerónimos, the monument to the discoveries, and the beaches of Costa da Caparica, where people multiply miraculously like ants around a cake, far from home, you shrivel up and die like a cactus in the polar regions. The subway tunnels are your real intestines, traveled by the dejecta of carriages, and the X-rays you can have taken in the free X-ray unit in Praça do Chile are the small-scale negatives of your soul. The thing that keeps us irremediably apart is that you only knew the names of those dead soldiers from the death notices in the newspapers, whereas I shared with them our army ration of fruit salad and saw their coffins being welded shut in the company depot, among the crates of munitions and rusty helmets. Corporal Pereira, for example, before he got his head blown off on the road to Chiquita, would come to the first-aid post to have his blennorrhea drained, his prick as limp as a stearin candle and dripping painful burning drops like inflamed milk. The baker wrote an autobiographical poem that took two hours to recite and sent me to sleep over my lunch out of sheer exhaustion. The lieutenant boasted to me about his maid's many qualities as ecstatically as if he were describing a miracle. The commander sought out the breasts, soft as grapes, of adolescent girls, rumpling their dresses. A captain in the fourth command was dissolving like a Dracula at dawn, his features decomposing into the pale mud of corpses. And I went from village to village with all the gravity of a village chief, I sat on the goatskin benches intended for high-ranking visitors, distributed quinine to long lines of trembling malaria sufferers, drained abscesses, disinfected wounds, and smoked marijuana as I watched the feverish dancers and wild-eyed men kneeling, shaking before the panicking hearts of the drums. In the jungle, the whites, isolated and with no means of keeping up their farms, would stash their weapons at the head of the bed and lie down next to their black mistresses, who lay there, as obedient and silent as the oblique shadow cast by a ghost. Like a thousand victorious, hungry, vegetable mouths, the scrub swallowed up the broken-down tractors, devoured houses, jumped over fences, destroyed the anonymous crosses in the graveyards scattered randomly along the jungle paths. One day, a blond man driving a ruin of a truck turned up at the barracks, got out, carrying a suitcase full of priest's vestments, and introduced himself to the officers in Spanish thus:

"I'm a Basque and a close friend of that bastard Francisco Franco."

In Gago Coutinho, there was an abandoned mission, an old building with a colonnade protected by the cool shade of acacias, an oasis of silence where your footsteps echoed like in a Hitchcock movie. In the afternoons, the lieutenant and I used to park the Jeep by the rusty iron railings, take out the back seat, and install ourselves beneath a tree to enjoy the plump peace of birdsong, the fine, spacious silence of lofty leaves, and we would sit there, smoking and not talking, because words suddenly became as unnecessary as a boat in the city, an aquarium in the sea, a fake orgasm during orgasm, we smoked and didn't talk and a tranquil stillness slipped slowly into our veins, reconciled us to ourselves, and made us able to forgive ourselves for being there, the involuntary occupiers of a foreign land, the agents of a provincial form of Fascism that was corroding and eating away at itself with the slow acid of its own sad, parochial stupidity.

"I'm a Basque and a close friend of that bastard Francisco Franco."

In Dala-Samba, the administrator lived with his wife and children in an empty house and from the verandah you could see the whole vast blue extent of Cassanje and the frontier with the Congo, and down below, the diamond-bright river sending flakes of light bouncing off the smooth stones. His children, who suffered from worms, writhed in pain on the verandah. His wife crocheted for weeks on end, slippers and oval doilies in which one sensed a lost Campo de Ourique with its constellation of shops selling cheap trinkets gathered around the Igreja do Santo Condestável, a construction in Disneyland Gothic where technocrats got married. The oil lamp illuminated a Georges de La Tour supper, where the faces resembled attentive apples set against a shifting backdrop of shadows, while the village next door, turned in upon itself like a meditating philosopher, withdrew into the darkness with its sparse fires and crouching silhouettes, as they roasted the wriggling crickets that were their supper.

"I'm a Basque. . . ."

Dammit, I came here too because I was driven from my country on board a ship crammed from the hold to the bridge with soldiers and was then imprisoned behind three rows of barbed wire surrounded by mines and war, they left me only the occasional oxygen bottle of a letter from my family and photographs of my daughter, Angola was a pink rectangle on a primary-school map, black nuns beaming out from a missionary calendar, women with rings through their noses, Mouzinho de Albuquerque,* and hippopotamuses, the heroism of the Portuguese Youth Movement marking time beneath the April rain in the school playground. A black friend from university days once took me to his room in Arco do Cego and showed me the photo of a skeletally thin old lady on whose face one could see generations and generations of petrified revolt:

"This is our *Guernica*. I wanted you to see it before I left because I've just received my draft papers and I'm deserting tomorrow to Tanzania."

And I only understood what he meant when I saw the prisoners

---

*Joaquim Augusto Mouzinho de Albuquerque (1855–1902) was a Portuguese soldier who pacified Mozambique. Highly regarded in the Portugal of the nineteenth and twentieth centuries, he was seen as a symbol of Portuguese reaction to threats against Portugal's African colonies from the more powerful northern European empires, such as Britain.

in the PIDE headquarters, their look of resignation as they waited, the distended, malnourished bellies of their children, the absence of tears in their terrified eyes. You have to understand, you see, that in the world into which I was born the definition of a black was "a cute little thing when small," the way you might refer to a dog or a horse, to some strange, dangerous animal with a curious resemblance to humans, who in the darkness of Santo António village yelled at me:

"Go back to your own country, Portuguese"

not giving a shit about my vaccines and my medicines and hoping desperately that I got my brains blown out on the road back because I wasn't treating *them*, but the farmers' cheap labor, seventeen *escudos* a day, ten *tostões* per sack of cotton, I was treating the white man in Malanje or Luanda, the white man lying in the sun on Luanda Island, the white man in the smart residential area of Alvalade in Lisbon, the white man in the local sports club, who scornfully refused to talk to soldiers

"We don't need *you*"

and so my friend's *Guernica* gradually became my *Guernica* too, just as I became "a Basque and a close friend of that bastard Francisco Franco" and put my vaccines and my medicines back in the box and returned to the wire fences and the mango trees of Marimba, reached the first-aid post, closed the door, sat down at my desk, and suddenly, how can I put it, I felt like a hunted beast.

S

I told the person in the living room that I would be right back, Sofia, and then I came in here and sat down on the toilet opposite the mirror where I shave every morning, so that I could talk to you. I miss your smile, your hands on my body, your feet tickling my feet. I miss the lovely smell of your hair. In the oblique light from the ceiling lamp, this bathroom is an aquarium of tiles run aground in the water of the night and in it my face moves with the slow, rippling gestures of a sea anemone, my arms wave spasmodically like the boneless farewells of octopuses, while my body is relearning the white immobility of coral. When I lather up my face, Sofia, I can feel the glass scales of my skin on my fingers, my eyes resemble the sad, bulging eyes of the sea bream on the kitchen table, angel fins are sprouting from my armpits. I am dissolving, motionless, in the full bathtub, as I imagine fish do when they die in rivers, evaporating into a sticky foam, their putrefying eyes bobbing about on the surface. Here, Sofia, dawn after dawn, when the morning has not yet outlined the rooftops in green, and the lights still stand out clearly in the dark like phosphorescent warts, when the ample shadows of Lisbon wrap me in their soft, terrifying folds, I come into the bathroom, propelled by the enormous hand of the mother I no longer have, in order to offer up a child's furtive trickle of pee. Now that I'm a man, Sofia, I live alone and the concierge greets me with a respectful bow, yet sometimes I'm still assailed by the strange certainty that I'm a dead fish floating in this aquarium of tiles, carrying out a daily ritual between the mirror and the bidet in the same lackluster way in which the dead, perhaps, move around beneath the earth, staring at each other with eyes full of inexpressible horror. I miss your belly pressed against mine, the forest of your black thighs twined about mine, your warm, loud, mysterious laughter whose joyful, victorious cascade remained intact despite the PIDE, the government, the CETEC tractor drivers, the administrator's greed, and the perverse, sadistic fury of the whites. I miss your bed where I could take my long European rest with eight centuries of stone *infantas* on my shoulders, I miss your sun-warm vagina in which I could anchor my embarrassingly tender feelings, I miss my erect penis bending toward you as the mast of a ship bends into the wind, I miss the furious thirst for love that I dared not show you, Sofia. I settle myself on the toilet like a hen getting ready to lay, shaking my shaggy, feathered buttocks on the plastic halo of the toilet seat, until I release one golden egg that leaves in the bowl an ochre smear of shit, I flush the toilet and cackle like any other contented layer of eggs, and it's as if that melancholy feat justified my whole existence, as if sitting here, night after night, opposite the mirror, observing in the glass the sallow bags beneath my eyes and the lines around my mouth, which are multiplying to form a fine mysterious web identical to the cross-hatching in Leonardo's drawings, as if sitting here assured me that, after all the years that have passed since I left you, I am still alive, I still survive, Sofia, in this

aquarium of tiles lit obliquely by the ceiling light, a dead fish floating on the surface, my putrefying eyes bobbing about.

I met you in Gago Coutinho one Saturday morning, the time
when the washerwomen came to the wire fence to deliver the soldiers' starched and ironed clothes and crouched, waiting, on a slope
near the dislocated barrier of the sentry post, speaking a strange
language I could barely understand, which sounded rather like
Charlie Parker's saxophone when he's not screaming out his
wounded hatred for the cruel, ridiculous world of the white man.
We found the putrid smell of Africa's red earth as nauseating as the
smell of the dead in the hospital, while the insects of Eastern Angola
busily devoured each other in the silence of the scrub, and the washerwomen, with their bundles of laundered clothes wrapped in colorful cloth, allowed the soldiers to run their hands over waist, back,
breasts, beneath the huge, dense, fixed sun of Angola, meanwhile
chatting to each other and mocking the greedy desire of these white
men, their clumsiness and their haste, and also the corpselike smell
they brought with them from the Lisbon ship, men transformed
into larvae equipped with murderous rifles, sent there by a Portugal full of policemen.

On Saturday mornings, the old men would gather in the middle
of the village around a gourd full of tobacco and sit there, puffing
away like steam engines, sending out serene, brown clouds of
smoke, their hatred of the occupying force written in large red letters on their vegetable indifference. They were the old men of
Nengo, of Lusse, of Luate, the old men of Cessa and Mussuma, the
old men of Luanguinga and Lucusse, the old men of Narriquinha,
the old men of Chalala, the proud old Luchazi, masters of this Land
at the End of the World, who, many centuries earlier, had arrived in
successive migrations from Ethiopia and driven out the Hottentots,

the Kamessekeles, the people who inhabited that land of sand and cold nights, where the bushes trembled when the phosphorescent ghosts of gods brushed past them. These were free men enslaved by the barbed wire and by the *canhangulos*—the primitive rifles—of the black militiamen, by the angry, triangular, lizard faces of PIDE agents, by the rancorous colonial State that treated them like an ignoble race, old men who spat out onto the dark earth their smoking, tobacco-stained saliva in great heavy gobs of scorn.

The old men gathered in the central meeting place, barking dogs chased the scrawny hens from village to village, and a light, almost imperceptible pollen—similar to the dust that emanated from the old boxes of rouge that accumulated in the warped drawers of the closets of my childhood—fell from trees as still as stones, putting down strange basalt roots in the crazy African earth. In his armored office, the commander shrugged his shoulders, for he, too, was a slave of the barbed wire and of the proud, inhuman masters of war, who, safe in Luanda, were busy sticking colored pins in maps and slowly killing us one by one, and I looked at you, Sofia, crouched on the bank among the green, blue, and black stain of the women talking and laughing and making fun of the soldiers' fingers anxiously touching them, the Luchazi women who opened their indifferent vulvas to white men, in huts full of the humid silence of their mute offspring, who sat in one corner playing with bits of sugarcane, playing the solemn games of children.

I met you one Saturday morning, Sofia, and your laugh, the laugh of a free prisoner, as strange and harmonious as the flock of crows Van Gogh painted just before he shot himself in the middle of the wheat and the sun, touched me in the way that a gesture of irrepressible tenderness always touches me if I'm feeling particularly alone, or as the whispering ghosts in our house in Benfica always touched me, that house near the cemetery, surrounded by the sweet, sad laments of the dead.

I was sick of war, Sofia, of the enduring evil of war and of listening, in bed, to the protests of my murdered comrades who pursued me in my sleep, pleading with me not to let them rot inside their lead coffins, as cold and troubling as the gaunt shapes of olive trees, I was sick of being a larva among other larvae in the funeral chamber of the officers' mess intermittently lit by the electricity generator's swooning, hesitant vacillations, sick of playing checkers with the aging captains and sick of the second lieutenants' melancholy jokes, sick of working, night after night, in the infirmary, up to my elbows in the hot, viscous blood of the wounded. I was sick of it all, Sofia, and my whole body was begging me for the peace that can be found only in the serene bodies of women, in the curve of a woman's shoulder on which I could rest my despair and fear, in that tenderness devoid of sarcasm, in that sweet generosity, as welcoming as a cradle to my male anxiety, the hate-laden anxiety of a man alone, with the unbearable weight of my own death on my back. The medic, who had the pale, prominent eyes of a blind horse and a terrible fear of Africa in his guts, dragged you over by one arm, a dark, round, firm young arm, to the place along the barbed-wire fence, opposite the white road into Luso, where I had stopped to look at you and, beyond you, at the verdigris expanse of the jungle that the stupid tractors were demolishing, trunk by trunk, and he asked me in a sorrowful voice, just like an antenna shyly withdrawing as if it had taken fright at itself, the same voice with which my murdered comrades called to me in my sleep, their heads swathed in bandages as useless as rags flapping about wet, disheveled locks, the voice of my dog who died years before, sniffing around the fig tree in the garden, and who was now just the echo of a howl evaporating from my memory:

"Do you need a washerwoman, sir?"

I didn't need a washerwoman, Sofia, because the stretcher bearers dealt with my shirts and towels and pants and socks, but I did need you, I needed the fruit smell of your belly, your tattooed pubis, the string of beads tight around your waist, your long, hard feet like those of some river bird, striding nervously, majestically, from stone to stone.

I was sick of the war, Sofia, sick of seeing more wounded men arriving from the jungle on improvised canvas stretchers, the wounded whose mouths opened and closed uttering cries as mournful and indecipherable as the call of the sea, the sea at Praia das Maçãs that came to roar at my sheets like some bull in heat, blowing out through its nostrils the boiling foam of waves. Above the pharmacy, my brothers and I, huddled in the damp sheets like frightened fetuses, would lie awake and listen uncomprehendingly to the sea's gruff language, to the bull of the sea butting at the bedroom door, jumping over the wall and running full tilt through the streets, then resting its vast, cold snout on the pillow next to us in order to try to sleep, because the sea, Sofia, suffers from the same persistent insomnia as the dead who used to make the floorboards creak at the house in Benfica with their unbearable, gaseous steps.

I was sick of the war, of spending all night, into the small hours, bent over my dying comrades, beneath the vertical light of the improvised operating room, I was sick of the blood so cruelly spilled, sick of going outside before dawn to smoke a cigarette in the deep dark of night that precedes the day, in the deep, dense, limitlessly dark night that precedes the day, and suddenly seeing the serene vault of the sky dotted with unfamiliar stars, not the Benfica sky of lavender and naphthalene, nor the hard sky of granite pines in Beira, not even the sky of stormy waters in Praia das

Maçãs on which one sailed like a boat adrift, but the high, serene, unreachable sky of Africa and its geometric constellations that glittered ironically, like eyes. Standing at the door of the operating room, with the barracks dogs sniffing at my clothes, greedy for the blood of my wounded comrades, licking their blood from the dark stains on my trousers, my shirt, the fair hair on my arms, Sofia, I hated the people who were lying to us and oppressing us and humiliating and killing us in Angola, the serious, dignified gentlemen in Lisbon stabbing those of us in Angola in the back, the politicians, magistrates, policemen, informers, and bishops, who, to the sound of hymns and speeches, herded us onto warships and packed us off to Africa, sent us off to die in Africa and then wove sinister, vampirish melodies around us.

After supper on the night of the day when I met you, I escaped the wives of the aged captains and the lieutenants' game of poker, shooed away the dogs reduced to prowling around the mess in ellipses of stubborn, submissive hunger now that the villagers were competing with them for the mice, those small, eager, timid beasts of the field sniffing anxiously at our white man's shadows, and I walked past the sentry post and headed toward the vague dark stain of the village down below, from where the smell of manioc rose up like a breath from the grave, the manioc drying on the roofs of the huts and looking just like the bones that Senhor Joaquim, who sold skeletons to the medical students, bought from the gravedigger in Alto de São João in Lisbon and left to dry in his attic room in Campo de Santana, gently polluting the sad, urban odor of the trees in the garden.

I could have sworn you were waiting for me, Sofia, on the other side of those thick adobe walls that still preserved, in the hard mud, the prints of the anonymous fingers that had built them, because the wooden door opened without my even touching it, opened onto a darkness even darker than the dark of the night, but peopled with the silence of breathings and whispers, with the soft cackle of sleeping hens, with the fugitive back of a dog, with your hand, Sofia, that guided me in the gloom, yes, you guided me through the darkness and the silence just as, one day, when I'm blind, my daughter will guide me, and I could sense the victorious chuckle on your lips, the laughter of a free woman whom no PIDE agent, no soldier, no *cipaio* could silence, a laughter I can still hear, even today, in this loathsome, aseptic aquarium of tiles, as I sit on the toilet, looking in the mirror at a face grown irremediably older, my fingers yellow with nicotine, the gray hairs I didn't have before, the wrinkles, Sofia, that mark my brow with the listlessness of those who have definitively given up all hope.

I could have sworn that the hollow in your straw mattress was the exact shape of my body, as if you had been patiently waiting for me from the start, that the size of your vagina was, miraculously, the perfect size for my penis, that the mulatto child snoring in the raffia cradle, the boy whom the redheaded, adenoidal storekeeper, Alfonso, claimed as his own and received from time to time, with a scornful slap, in his narrow shop that stank of dried fish, I could have sworn that the boy's face in repose had something of my face before the bitterness and suffering of war had transformed me into this cynical, disenchanted creature, mechanically performing the act of love with the indifferent, distracted gestures of someone eating alone in a restaurant, gazing inside himself at the melancholy ghosts that inhabit him.

You were waiting for me, Sofia, in the dense night of your hut in the village, you lit the wick of an improvised oil-lamp, and the faint, dull, winking light revealed to me, here and there, cans on shelves, a basket of clothes, the closed square of a window, an old lady crouched, perfectly still, in one corner, smoking her cane pipe, a very old old lady with hair whiter than the cotton in Cassanje, with flat, empty breasts that clung to her ribs the way the eyelids of the dead stick to their empty sockets. You were waiting for me, Sofia, and we never needed any words, because you understood my male anxiety, the hate-laden anxiety of a man alone, the indignation I felt at my own cowardice, at my submissive acceptance of the violence and the war that those gentlemen in Lisbon had imposed on me, you understood my desperate caresses and my fearful tenderness, and your arms moved slowly down my back, with no anger and no sarcasm, moved slowly up and down over the cold sweat covering my skin, slowly pressed my head against your curved shoulder, and I was certain, Sofia, that, in the darkness, you had on your face the silent, mysterious smile that women smile when men suddenly become boys again and surrender to them like vulnerable, fragile children, exhausted from battling the things in themselves that disgust them.

Your house, Sofia, smelled of something alive, of something as joyful and alive as your sudden laughter, something warm and healthy and delicate and invincible, and to me, coming as I did from the barracks and the desperate bitterness of the other officers sick of killing and seeing people die, beset as I was by the painful colic of longing and fear, being with you tasted of childhood, tasted of Gija's nails gently scratching my back, of my grandfather bending over my sleeping self and planting the violet of a kiss on my forehead, it tasted of my Aunt Madalena calling me Dear child and stroking my hair, me, who spent all my time in my room, disdainfully alone, occasionally looking out at the fig tree in the garden and feeling in my guts the feverish spores of a searing inner isolation.

Because, you see, I was always alone, Sofia, during primary school, college, university, hospital, marriage, alone with the books I had read far too many times and with my own vulgar, pretentious poems, with the longing to write and the tormenting fear that I couldn't, that I wouldn't be able to translate into words what I wanted to bellow into the ears of others: I'm here, Notice me, I'm here, Listen to me and understand me even when I'm silent, but you see, Sofia, what isn't said can't be understood, people look but don't understand, they go away, they talk to each other at a distance from us, oblivious to us, and then we feel like a beach in autumn, empty of footprints, on which the sea advances and then retreats with the involuntary motion of a lifeless arm. I was always alone, Sofia, even in the war, especially in the war, because the camaraderie of war is based on a false generosity, composed of an unavoidable common fate endured together but never really shared, lying in the same shelter while the mortars explode like the shrapnel-filled bellies of the men dying in the infirmary, pointing our sharp noses, like doomed birds, at the ceiling, yes, alone, even in the abandoned mission, sitting with the lieutenant on the back seat of the Jeep under the acacias, listening to the insects and the birds and the deafening silence of Africa, alone in the infirmary in the middle of all those wounded men, who moaned and wept and called to me for nights on end, bent double with fear and pain. What an imbecilic war, Sofia. I can say that now, crouched on the toilet in front of the pitiless mirror that is slowly aging me, beneath this aquarium light and among these glazed tiles, these bottles, these smooth metal and ceramic bathroom fittings, what an imbecilic war we were fighting in that burning, miraculous Africa that made you feel like springing up out of the earth the way the sunflowers, the rice, the cotton, and the children surged upward with the impetus of a geyser, steaming and triumphant.

Why is it, Sofia, that black women remain silent when they give birth, silent and serene on their mats while the head of their child pushes slowly out from the space between their thighs, takes shape, breaks free, a shoulder disengages itself from the fold of the womb containing it, the trunk slides out of the vagina like a penis after coitus, in one smooth, implacable, painless movement, the gentle separation of two lives, the simple distancing of two bodies that will never again come together, just like us, Sofia, we, too, lost each other, and when I went to your house and the door didn't open, I scratched on the wood with my nails, I prowled around the adobe walls, listening, and an empty muteness answered me, no breathing, no gentle cackle from the sleeping hens through the gaps and cracks in the mud, through the combed grass of the roof, I scratched again on the wooden door, and the old woman with the pipe in her mouth opened up and slid me a stony look, the cloth covering her withered belly fluttered a little, I went over and peered inside, a lit taper illuminated the deserted bed, the calcareous folds of the sheets, the rusty cans on the shelf, the awful hollow of absence. The old woman took the pipe out of her mouth like someone struggling to unstick a stamp from an envelope, aimed a gob of spit as dark as a rain cloud at my thigh (the concentric folds around her puckered mouth reminded me of an anus), then blew a tremulous volute of smoke into the air and said:

"PIDE took her."

She could have been your mother or possibly your grandmother, yet there was no apparent feeling of sorrow or alarm in her voice, or, if there was, I didn't notice, astonished as I was to hear her speak, as astonished as if a chair or a table had suddenly launched into a booming recitation of one of my father's favorite sonnets by Antero de Quental.

The following day, on my way to the civilian hospital, I passed by the PIDE headquarters, where the prisoners were hoeing the agents' fields under the fierce vigilance of an armed prison guard, who was leaning against the wall in the shade of the house like a hyena ready to pounce, keeping watch over the thin, near-naked, shaven-headed men and women, their bodies swollen from kicks and slaps, who were bending toward the earth with the limp gestures of bodies soon to be corpses. I walked into the PIDE headquarters, Sofia, I went through the door, shaking with fear and disgust, and I asked the brigade chief what had happened to you, he was standing next to his Land Rover giving orders to two pale-complexioned creatures with pistols in their belts, who were taking careful notes in the kind of spiral-bound notebook we used at school. The bastard chuckled with contentment, like a friar at a banquet.

"She was a bit of all right, eh? Unfortunately, she was in with the kaffirs, so we gave her the once-over, just so the boys could have a bit of an oil change, know what I mean, then issued her a one-way ticket to Luanda."

I have to go back in now, Sofia. It's almost morning and the whisky is evaporating through the walls of my body like breath on a windowpane, leaving me to struggle painfully against the disenchanted brightness of dawn, in which the wind of the vacant years is breathing through its exhausted nose, making a sound transparent with sadness. The tree of my blood is reaching out along the countless, numb branches of my limbs, spreading a mist over my skin as melancholy as the November mist in Lisbon, my battered, humble city, which is waking up, house by house, to another very ordinary day. And I leave this aquarium of tiles just as I left the PIDE headquarters, where the prisoners were hoeing the agents' fields, bending toward the earth with the limp gestures of cadavers, and I still didn't have the courage to cry out in indignation or revolt, I will finish this night as I did then, without protest, after twenty-seven months of bloody slavery, I go into the corridor, Sofia, I turn out the light, and I start to smile the pious, joyless smile of that bastard, the brigade chief, standing by the Land Rover, revealing his great smug hyena teeth. Because that's what I have become, that's what they have made of me, Sofia, a cynical, prematurely old creature laughing at himself and at others with the bitter, cruel, envious laughter of the dead, the silent, sadistic laughter of the dead, the repulsive, oily laughter of the dead, and all the while I'm rotting away inside, by the light of the whisky I've drunk, just as the photos in albums rot, regretfully, dissolving very slowly into a blur of mustaches.

I

*N*o, seriously, wait, let me undo your bra. One of the lights on the bedside table goes out, and a modest veil of shadow descends over the sheets like the veils that covered the faces of the earnest, anonymous ladies of my childhood who came to offer condolences and sat around a silver teapot, drinking solemn cups of tea and lightly brushing the plates of cookies with their suede-gloved fingers. I sit on the bed to take off my socks, while you struggle with the zipper on your pants, as impatient as a taxi driver at a red light, and maybe, with a little luck, the room will fill with a gentle conjugal atmosphere composed of a web of patiently acquired shared habits. But please, let me undo your bra: I love the small, complicated fastenings that always open the opposite way from what you expect, and the breasts that, finally, leave in my hand their cloth envelope, just as snakes drape their discarded skins on trees. Have you noticed how breasts emerge like moons from clothes, round, white, soft, opaline, with a warm inner light of veins and milk, rising above the city of my body in slow triumph? I like the way breasts perform a kind of flanking maneuver and rise indifferently to the tremulous, eager height of my kisses, I like to cover their calm softness with the cloud of one arm, to bend over the aureole of their nipples with all the clumsy care of an astronaut and rest my head in the hollow between them and feel inside me, my eyes closed, the deep tranquillity of a sea finally in repose, touched very lightly by the hesitant halo of a dawning breast.

Lying beside you, beside your bare shape, motionless as the dead, your thighs spread on the sheets, the touching, fragile, geometric little forest of your pubis, whose reddish hairs, in the light from the bedside lamp, stand out as clearly and precisely as the branches of poplars at dusk, I am reminded of the soldier in Mangando who lay down on his bunk, put his gun to his neck, and said Goodnight, and how the lower half of his face then disappeared in a horrible roar, jaw, mouth, nose, and left ear, pieces of cartilage and bone and blood embedded in the corrugated iron roof like jewels in a ring, and how he took four hours to die in the first-aid post, writhing in agony despite repeated injections of morphine, a thick, sticky liquid bubbling up out of the gaping hole of his throat.

When I heard about the shot over the radio, I was sitting in the village meeting place in Marimba, next to the house of the narrow-hipped teacher who suffered such painful, interminable periods, and I was watching the night and the fantastic insects that inhabit the dense African dark and that the shadows tirelessly secrete and expel. When I heard about the shot over the radio, the umbrella-ribbed bats were whirling around like bits of paper in the wind beneath the vast wall of mango trees, Baixa do Cassanje was an Alentejo grown misty with ardent enthusiasm, with the furious joy of Angola, where even suffering and death take on the triumphant resonance of victory. A guy in Mangando has just shot himself, the medic was stuffing syringes and other instruments into a bag, the escort was already waiting for us near the sergeants' mess, and we went bumping off along the road heading north, waking up the owls that were sleeping, hunched, along the path and that flapped their wings in the headlights, much as a drowning man, so near to shore, might wave his arms in an anxious fluster of feathers.

Mangando, Marimbanguengo, Bimbe, and Caputo, there you have the cardinal points of my anxiety: Bimbe and Caputo were villages deep in the jungle, policed by militiamen and the so-called Special Groups, spied on by PIDE informers and by white volunteers, a sort of lay police force, dressed like the hippo and elephant hunters in the picture books of my childhood, books I found in Uncle Elói's attic that showed men with hunting boots and double-barreled shotguns, posing with one foot on the gray hulk of some dead animal. From the attic window, I could see the prison of Monsanto, which I imagined to be full of unshaven, wild-eyed, simian creatures shaking the bars, and whose breath, if I woke in the middle of the night, I thought I could feel right by my ear, a thought that left me paralyzed with fear. Uncle Elói used to wind the clocks and drink Anís El Mono out of a blue glass, and from the sideboard, as if from the face of a person one loves, there descended a sweet, timeless peace. Uncle Elói, I was thinking as we jolted down the road on our way to Mangando, summer afternoons in Benfica, as heavy as fruit murmurous with light, the hoarse voice of Chaby Pinheiro* issuing forth from the wind-up phonograph amid clicks and whistles, just where inside myself did I mislay that innocence? The car headlights wrenched the trees out of the darkness, sucking them violently toward us, the rain had gouged huge potholes out of the already rough road, in Bimbe and Caputo, the puppet chiefs, imposed on the tribes by the government, fearfully shut themselves

---

* Chaby Pinheiro (1873–1933) was a popular actor in the Portuguese theatre.

away and clung to their wives. The Fascists had made a lot of big mistakes in Africa, you see, big stupid mistakes, because, fortunately, Fascism is very stupid, mistakes stupid and cruel enough to turn on them and devour them, and one such mistake was replacing the real chiefs, the noble, proud, indomitable chiefs, with phony ones, whom the people scorned and despised, they might pretend to respect them when in the presence of smug whites, but in secret, they despised them and continued to obey the real authorities hidden in the jungle, Chief Caputo, for example, seized the wooden image of the god Zumbi and vanished into the night, and his people, puzzled, contemplated the empty niche in great consternation and, each night, received instructions from the drums that throbbed and echoed in the darkness.

Mangando, Marimbanguengo, Bimbe, and Caputo: the troops stationed in Mangando and Marimbanguengo shook with malaria and fear, half-naked soldiers staggered about in the unbearable heat of the barracks, where the stench of sweat and unwashed bodies was as overwhelming as the nauseating breath of a corpse when you lean over it hoping to hear the sad, putrefying words that the dead pass on to the living in a babble of formless syllables. In Mangando and Marimbanguengo, I saw the full misery and evil of the war, the pointlessness of it all, in the soldiers' eyes, like those of wounded birds, in their state of despair and abandon, in the second lieutenant in shorts sprawled on the table, the stray dogs gobbling up leftovers on the parade ground, the flag hanging from the flagpole like a limp penis, I saw it in the twenty-year-old men sitting in the shade in silence, like old men in parks, and I said to the medic, who was disinfecting the guy's knee with iodine, One of these days the shit is really going to hit the fan, because when you get twenty-year-old men sitting in the shade like that, completely hopeless, something strange and unexpected and tragic is sure to happen, then they told me over the radio, A guy in Mangando has just shot himself, and I ran to the car where the escort was waiting for me, and we went bumping off along that potholed road heading north.

It's odd talking to you about this while touching your breasts, stroking your belly, fumbling for the moist junction between your thighs where the world truly begins, because it was there, emerging from between my mother's legs, that I first saw, with eyes as fresh as newly minted coins, the strange, whispering world of adults, its unease and its haste. It's odd talking to you about this in Lisbon, in this room papered with the floral print that a girlfriend chose before she disappeared, vanishing from my life as suddenly and obliquely as she arrived and leaving in my guts a kind of wound that still hurts when I touch it, in this room from where you can see the river, the lights of Almada and Barreiro, the heavy, phosphorescent blue of the water. So strange that sometimes I wonder if the war really did end or if it's still going on somewhere inside of me, with its disgusting smells of sweat and gunpowder and blood, its dislocated bodies, its waiting coffins. I think that when I die, colonial Africa will come back to meet me and then I will search in vain, in the niche of the god Zumbi, for wooden eyes that are no longer there, I will see again the Mangando barracks dissolving in the heat, the blacks from the village in the distance, the sleeve of the landing strip waving mockingly at no one. Once again, it will be night and I will step down from the Unimog taking me to the first-aid post, where the man with no face is dying, lit by the kerosene lamp that a corporal is holding at head height and on which the bodies of flying insects sizzle and crack.

The man with no face is dying in a state of uncontrollable agitation, tied to the treatment table that wobbles and shakes and seems about to collapse with every lurching movement, its leprous, rusty joints groaning. Curious noses press against the windows, a small cluster of fascinated, panic-stricken people gathers at the door to watch the blood and saliva that bubble up out of that nonexistent throat, to hear the indefinable sounds that emerge from what remains of the nose, to see the eyes that the gunpowder burst like two exploded boiled eggs. The ampules of morphine injected into the deltoid muscle seem only to make his bound body rock and writhe even more, and the kerosene lamp multiplies these movements on the walls in the form of shadows that interpenetrate, then move apart, creating a frenetic dance on the stained and grubby geometry of the stucco. I feel like flinging open the door and leaving, stumbling over any stray dogs and frightened children who might wind themselves about my legs, and breathing in the damp cotton-batting air of Africa, sitting on the steps of the old settler's house, my chin cupped in my hands, feeling quite empty now of indignation, remorse, or pity, remembering my daughter's pale eyes in the photos they send me from Lisbon, and imagining myself watching over her sleep, bent over the covers in her crib, touched and concerned. The crickets in Mangando fill the night with noises, a grave, long-drawn-out, continuous song rises up from the earth, the trees, the bushes, the miraculous flora of Africa let go of the earth and float free into that dense atmosphere of vibrations and whispers, the guy tied to the bed is dying just three feet away from me like the crucified frogs pinned onto corkboards at school ready for dissection, I keep injecting ampule after ampule of morphine into the muscle in his arm, wishing I were eight thousand miles from there and watching over my sleeping daughter in her crib, wishing I had never been born to see such a thing, the idiotic, colossal pointlessness of it all, wishing I were in Paris fomenting revolutions in a café somewhere or studying in London and talking about my country with the awful provincial irony of an Eça de Queiroz, speaking about my rabble of a country to my English, French, Swiss, Portuguese friends, who had never felt in their blood the intense, pungent fear of dying, never seen bodies blown apart by mines or bullets. The captain with the wire-rimmed spectacles kept saying inside my head, The revolution is made from within, and I was looking at the soldier with no face and trying to quell the wave of bile rising up from my stomach, and I wished I were studying economics or sociology or whatever the fuck else in Vincennes, waiting tranquilly, all the while despising my country, waiting for the murdered to liberate it, for those who had been slaughtered in Angola to drive out the cowardly scum enslaving my country, and then to make my return, competent, grave, wise, sardonic, and a Social Democrat to boot, carrying with me in my trunkful of books the glib cleverness of the latest paper truth.

Mangando, Marimbanguengo, Bimbe, and Caputo: the guy finally stopped moving after one final convulsion, what was left of his throat ceased its desperate bubbling, and the corporal holding the kerosene lamp lowered his arm and the shadow lay down on the floor in doglike shame, suddenly still. We stood for a long time studying that body now at rest, his hands lightly curled on his thighs, his boots seemingly filled with straw, motionless on the chipped white paint of the bed. Those watching through the windows vanished in the direction of the barracks, melted slowly away in an inaudible murmur, and I would have given anything to have been far from there, far from that dead guy silently accusing me, far from the pile of empty ampules of morphine in the dressing bucket with the gauze, cotton, and compresses, to be in Paris, explaining in a café how to combat Fascism, or in London addressing a lecture on Marcuse to the legs of some bedazzled English girl, or in Benfica running one finger over the sleeping head of my daughter, or reading Salinger with the curtains open to the fig tree in the garden, in which the night was getting tangled up just as my clumsy hands used to tangle my aunts' skeins of wool.

No. Not yet. Let me embrace you slowly, feel your skin on mine, the soft curve of your waist. I like the taste of your mouth, I like touching with my tongue the plaque on your teeth that speaks to me of your marvelous human perishability, I like to see how your eyelids close when your lips come near, to watch the easy surrender of your whole body. This bed is an island adrift in Lisbon's sea of buildings and rooftops, our hair the wispy leaves of the palm trees in the wind, our hands reaching out to each other an eager putting-down of roots. When your knees gently part, when your elbows press against my ribs, when your reddish pubis opens its flesh petals in a moist surrender of warm, soft valves, I will enter you like a humble, mangy dog curling up on a landing to sleep, hoping for some impossible comfort from the cold wood, because the guy in Mangando and all the other guys in Mangando and Marim-banguengo and Cessa and Mussuma and Ninda and Chiúme will rise up inside me in their lead coffins, wrapped in their fluttering, blood-stained bandages, demanding, in the resigned, mournful tones of the dead, what, out of fear, I never gave them: a cry of revolt, a refusal to submit to the gentlemen running the war in Lisbon, the same gentlemen who, holed up in the barracks at Carmo, shamelessly shat themselves and wept, mad with panic, on the day of their wretched defeat, faced by the triumphant sea of people dragging with them, in their urgent song, like the Tagus itself, the scrawny trees in the square. The guys in Marimba who refused to go to the refectory, refused to eat, and stayed in their

lines on the parade ground, with the longest-serving corporal
beside them, a serious, fair-haired man of few words, standing at
attention until the officer on duty, right in front of me, struck him
with his pistol, the corporal fell but got up and again stood at attention, blood flowing from nose, eyebrows, mouth, the rest of the
company staring straight ahead, the officer was kicking the man
now as he was down on all fours trying to recover his beret and put
it on, a body that kept repeating with stubborn, indestructible
patience, Yessir, Yessir, Yessir, and finally the company marched
slowly over to the refectory and accepted the slops that passed for
supper. It wasn't the food that was in question, you see, we all ate
the same putrid mush that the village children, armed with rusty
cans, yearned for, their great, hollow, hungry eyes hovering
beseechingly by the wire fence, it was the war, the stupidity of that
war, the unchanging calendars full of interminable days, as long
and deep as the sad, gentle smiles of lonely women, it was the silhouettes of our murdered comrades prowling the barracks at night,
talking to us in the pale-yellow voices of the dead, fixing us with the
same wounded, accusing gaze as the skeletal stray dogs that accompanied us. The soldiers believed in me, they saw me working in the
infirmary on bodies torn apart by mines, they saw me standing
beside their bunk when they were shaking with malarial fever in
their tangled sheets, so they felt I was one of them, ready to support
them in their angry protests, they saw me go into the barracks
where a man, barricaded in, was brandishing a large sword and
threatening to kill everyone and himself, and they saw how,
moments later, he followed me out, sobbing on my shoulder like an
oversize baby, the soldiers, therefore, thought me capable of accompanying them in their struggle, of fighting for them and joining
forces with their ingenuous hatred of the gentlemen in Lisbon, who

continued to fire the poisoned bullets of their patriotic speeches at us, but instead, sickened, they watched my utter passivity, my arms hanging by my side, my complete absence of combativeness and courage, my resignation to my fate as a prisoner.

Wait a moment, let me embrace you slowly, feel the beating of your veins against my belly, the growing wave of desire that spreads, singing, over the skin, our legs pedaling eagerly in the sheets, waiting. Let the room fill with the sound of faint moans in search of a mouth in which to anchor. Let me return from Africa to here and feel happy, almost happy, stroking your buttocks, your back, your soft, cool inner thigh, firm and tender as a fruit. Let me forget, by looking at you, what I can't forget, the murderous violence in that pregnant land of Africa, and then receive me inside you when my round, frightened eyes, sullied now with desire, become, instead, on this Lisbon morning, the hollow, hungry gaze of the village children hovering by the wire fence and holding out their rusty cans to your white breasts.

U

---

*H*ow was it for you? Only so-so? Sorry, I'm not in shape today, I feel awkward, distant, not in control of my body, the whisky has polluted my breath with an aftertaste of urine, I'm too painfully aware of my own inadequacies. For many years, I considered subscribing to one of those courses advertised in pamphlets that arrive in the mail and that claim, in only two weeks, to transform you into an efficient, well-groomed, clean-shaven Hercules, bulging with muscles and surrounded by an admiring cloud of dazzled young women:

JUST TEN MINUTES OF EXERCISE A DAY—AT HOME, NO EQUIPMENT REQUIRED—CAN MAKE *YOU* A REAL MAN.

IMPRESS YOUR BOSS AND THE LADIES WITH THE SAMSON WEIGHT-TRAINING METHOD.

BE FIVE INCHES TALLER WITHOUT THE NEED FOR LIFTS IN YOUR SHOES—TRY THE GULLIVER TECHNIQUE FOR LENGTHENING YOUR SHINBONES.

RESTORE YOUR HAIR TO ITS NATURAL COLOR WITH *JET LOTION*—JUST ONE APPLICATION IS ALL IT TAKES TO ACHIEVE SHINY, SILKY, SOFT HAIR.

ANXIOUS? DEPRESSED? FIVE LESSONS IN ASTRAL MAG-
NETISM WILL HAVE YOU LOOKING TO THE FUTURE WITH
CONFIDENCE.

LOSE THAT UNSIGHTLY BELLY BY CYCLING AT HOME
ON THE ABDOMOBIKE.

CAN'T FIND A JOB? COMBAT BALDNESS WITH HIRSU-
TEX, THE BIOLOGICAL OIL RICH IN SEAWEED NUTRIENTS,
AND ALL DOORS WILL OPEN TO YOU.

AFRAID TO GO TO THE BEACH BECAUSE YOU'RE
ASHAMED OF YOUR NARROW SHOULDERS? VISIT ANY
REPUTABLE CHEMIST AND ASK FOR A COPY OF OUR
EXPLANATORY LEAFLET: "HOW I WON MY WIFE'S HEART,
THANKS TO THE ELECTRONIC CLAVICULONE."

BAD BREATH? TRY NORWEGIAN CEBOLOV SPRAY (MADE
FROM ONION SKINS AND ESSENCE OF GARLIC) AND YOUR
FRIENDS WILL HANG ON YOUR EVERY WORD.

DO YOU STAMMER? PROFESSOR AZEREDO'S *PARAPSY-
CHOLOGICAL PSYCHOANALYSIS* WILL HAVE YOU SPEAKING AS
FLUENTLY AS ANY TV PRESENTER.

No, really, I'm only half-joking, mostly to disguise the humilia-
tion of failure and the disappointment threading its way through
your silence, like the shadows that now and then flit across my
youngest daughter's happy smile and that always awaken in the pit
of my stomach the acid of remorse and doubt. I would desperately
like to be different, to be someone capable of loving without embarrassment, to be someone my brothers could feel proud of, someone
I could feel proud of too, to be able to look in the mirror at the barber's or the tailor's and see reflected back a contented smile, fair

hair, a straight spine, a toned body beneath my clothes, as well as an unshakable sense of humor and a keen practical intelligence. I'm irritated by this clumsy, ugly envelope of mine, the phrases that get stuck in my throat, the not knowing what to do with my hands when I'm with strangers or people I find intimidating. I'm irritated by my fear of you, of displeasing you, of not being capable of making your body arch and undulate, at once victorious and vanquished, or of filling you with pleasure like an enormous wave just before it breaks so that, at the moment of orgasm, you speak the airy language of angels bestowing kisses in Latin. Please, let me try again, give my hopeless anguish one more chance, because I've given up all hope of trying to seduce you, of getting you to surrender to my sexual technique and my charm, of imagining you looking up my name in the phone book in order to ask me to supper next Saturday and sit gazing at me, oblivious to the roast beef and to time, with all the amazement of someone making a great discovery. It would be a chance not for you or for us, but for me: you could be my Electronic Claviculone of the soul and help me grow the broad shoulders of hope out of the skinny shoulder blades of despair, so that my suddenly triangular trunk can blithely raise up the defeated little man that I am. Carry me as some Herculean Pietà might carry a spent Christ, just as, years ago, I carried the black guy whose left leg had been bitten off by crocodiles in the River Cambo, and who was moaning softly, the way baby hyenas do in their stinking nests, surrounded by excrement and the white bones of gazelles.

I hated the River Cambo, that river of alligators and boa constrictors, because in the rainy season, its slow waters appeared to be the source of the great thunderclouds that advanced in dark billows toward the barracks, rolling the enormous pianos of the clouds down the stairways of the air. During those storms in Cassanje, we would all gather under the same corrugated iron roofs, trembling with fear, while an odor of phosphorus and sulfur floated in the ozone-saturated air and our stiff, blue hair sprouted skeins of sparks, while the trees, startled, bent humbly before the rain, because even the lofty trees of Angola grew small and fearful in the rain, and we would keep glancing at each other while the lightning fell, illuminating our faces with its magnesium flash and revealing beneath the skin the tragic outline of our cheekbones. On the banks of the River Cambo, I saw a boa constrictor die with a goat stuck in its throat, writhing on the grass the way patients suffering a heart attack writhed on hospital benches, sobbing and begging someone to kill them, trying to wrench out of their chests the veins vibrating inside them like the taut strings of a guitar. I saw the crocodiles' eyes drifting on the current, as thoughtful and intent as those of a young girl listening, blinking with the stony irony of certain busts of Voltaire, and beneath their apparent simplicity glimmered a carnivorous disdain for mankind. And I saw a hut struck by lightning, its roof as black as the dark, tragic eyelids of a flamenco dancer, and inside, sitting on a mat, a woman, utterly still, surrounded by the luminous green glow you find in plastic images of Our Lady of Fátima and on the hands of alarm clocks.

I hated the River Cambo and the scraggly bushes along its banks, the abandoned buildings with the colonnaded verandahs lost in the grass, and from whose ruins the lizards and the rats eyed us rancorously. We hated that river in which sad wooden gods called to each other in guttural voices full of appeals and threats, the river in which the washerwomen scrubbed our uniforms on the slimy stones, pursued by the constant hunger of the soldiers, who masturbated, kneeling on the ground, their weapons forgotten beside them. We had twenty-five months of war in our guts, twenty-five months of eating shit and drinking shit and fighting for shit and getting ill for shit and dying for shit, twenty-five interminable, painful, ridiculous months, so ridiculous that, sometimes, at night, in the village meeting place in Marimba, we would suddenly burst out laughing in each other's faces, explode in irrepressible guffaws, we would look at each other, and tears of pity, mockery, and anger would course down our thin cheeks, until the captain, gripping his empty cigarette holder between his teeth, would get into the Jeep and start sounding the horn, startling the bats and Angola's fantastical insects out of the mango trees, and then we would fall silent the way children suddenly do in the middle of a crying fit and we would stare into the surrounding darkness with a look of immense surprise.

We had twenty-five months of war in our guts, twenty-five months of senseless, imbecilic violence, and so we amused ourselves by biting each other the way animals do when they play, we would threaten each other with pistols, furiously insult each other like angry, envious dogs, we would roll around, barking, in the puddles left by the rain, we would put sleeping pills in our ration of whisky and then go staggering around the parade ground, shouting schoolboy obscenities. Days before, three of our comrades had died in an accident, a tree had unexpectedly stepped out of the jungle and planted itself vertically in the middle of the track, right in front of the Unimog in which they had set off from the store in Chiquita, after a few lukewarm beers, and we found their bodies scattered amid the scrub, their skulls fractured, with the red ants of Africa marching determinedly along their lifeless arms. Days before, our last murdered companions had left, wrapped in canvas, bound for the coffins in Malanje, which, even though they were made out of lead and wood, gave off a disgusting, fetid smell, and our comrades' dead faces, side by side in the barracks warehouse, had acquired a look of untroubled serenity, the amiable, distracted indifference of the young men I had forgotten they were, young men made old by unnecessary suffering. I envied them, you know, lying there among the sacks of potatoes and bags of flour, the bottles of soft drinks, the packs of cigarettes, the vast scales that looked like some medieval torture instrument, I envied their fearless tranquillity and the dull hope that seeped out from behind their barely closed eyelids, I envied them going back to Lisbon before me, bearing a flower of dried blood tattooed on their foreheads.

Listen. It'll be getting light soon, the barking of the dogs in the distant gardens has changed its tone slightly and taken on the pale, leaden echo of the dawn. Through the cracks in the blinds, the day is growing, as painful and swollen as a boil, sheltering inside it a pus of clocks and tiredness. There's a hint in the smoke from our cigarettes of the incense that lingers in churches after the ceremonies are over, among the pointed fingers of the candles and the painted virtue of the images, the beards dissolving beneath the soot of time on the panels of saints. It'll be getting light soon and all the lamps will be rendered redundant, the sun will pitilessly display our prone bodies, the wrinkles, the sad lines at the corners of our mouths, our disheveled hair, the traces of makeup on the pillow. Like a battlefield strewn with a disorder of corpses that no longer even arouse our pity, like an untidy attic in which the furniture has been replaced by ridiculous decapitated corpses. The muscular energy of the day is pushing us, like owls, into the last folds of darkness, where we anxiously, restlessly shake our damp feathers, huddled together in search of a nonexistent safety. Because no one will save us, no one can save us now, no company of soldiers will arrive, mortars at the ready, to find us. So here we are, utterly alone, without a compass, on the deck of this bed, bobbing about like a raft on the bedroom carpet. In a way, we are still in Angola, you and I, and I am making love to you as I did in the village of Macau in the hut belonging to Tia Teresa, a plump, wise, motherly black woman who received me on her straw mattress like a kindly, indulgent matron. Her fingers send shivers down my spine, her breath thick with fish and tobacco travels down my chest to my penis, which grows hard, and her huge, dark breasts, swollen with the transparent milk of kindness, sway before my mouth. The oil lamp reveals pious images, picture postcards stuck on the wall, the hairy lips of her vulva that brush my shoulder, like a barber's brush, hovering near my jacket, waiting for a tip, and I feel just like the dead men from the Unimog lying in the warehouse, with a flower of blood on my forehead, serene among the bags of flour and sacks of potatoes, the bottles of soft drinks and the packs of cigarettes. The officers are playing lotto in the administrator's house, the teacher with the painful periods is dancing around the dining table with the bus driver, a pallid colonial joy tinges every gesture with sadness, and Tia Teresa locks the door from the inside so that no one will disturb us and then she unbuttons my shirt with all the deliberate slowness of a ritual. Tia Teresa's village, surrounded by the sweet smell of marijuana and tobacco, is perhaps the only place that the war has not yet managed to fill with its cruel, pestilential stink. It spread throughout Angola, the scorched red earth of Angola, and reached Portugal on board the ships carrying the troops returning, disoriented and stunned, from an inferno of dust, it slipped into my humble city, which the gentlemen of Lisbon decked out in fake cardboard pomp, I found it lying in my daughter's crib, like a cat, fixing me with an oblique, malevolent stare, eyeing me from the sheets with the murky, envious rage of the second lieutenants at the card table, rancorously weighing up, pistols at their belts, the other players' cards. The war spread to the smiles of the women in the bars, beneath the grubby bulbs of lamps that filled with shadows the inquiring curves of their noses, it tainted the drinks with the sour taste of vengeance, it waited for us at the cinema, installed in our seats, wearing black like a widowed notary removing from his jacket pocket his plastic glasses case. It's here in this empty house, in the closets of this empty house, pregnant with the soft embryos of my underpants, in the geometric area of shadow that the lamps never reach, it's here and it calls to me softly with the pale, wounded voice of my comrades murdered on the roads of Ninda and Chiúme, it reaches out to me the white, bony elbows of a gauzy, tormenting embrace. It's in you, in your sarcastic, loveless profile, in your obstinate silence and in the mechanical movements of your buttocks during sex, devouring my penis with the blank indifference with which a stomach digests whatever food it's offered, receiving my kisses with the rather bored patience of the prostitutes of my youth, decrepit inflatable dolls anchored in the stains left on their mattresses by dried sperm. I squeeze half an inch of mentholated war onto my morning toothbrush and spit into the bowl the dark green foam of the eucalyptuses in Ninda, my beard is the jungle of Chalala resisting the napalm of my razor, a great murmur from the blood-soaked tropics grows in my protesting guts. But in Tia Teresa's hut, the air was sweetened by the marijuana leaves in a vase, the leaves that the soldiers brought back with them from Angola disguised in boxes of Band-Aids, to sell to the fragile young men in the Rossio, to the young men in the Rossio, who, like sickly birds, limp timidly, perversely, slowly around the fountains, in Tia Teresa's hut, when the door was locked and the bolts drawn on that intimate shrinelike silence, the war outside paced from mango tree to mango tree, leading by the hand its dead heroes and its false patriotism made of stucco and plaster, not daring to enter. Lying on the straw mattress, I would listen to its frantic pacing and know that it was peering through the cracks at my narrow, weary body, I sensed its silent, angry resentment at being shut out, spurned by the oil lamp, by the pious images and the picture postcards stuck on the wall, and I would smile, facedown on the pillow, because I was safe, safe and at peace in a country that was burning.

Listen. It'll be getting light soon, the alarm clocks in the buildings opposite will brutally propel the sleepers out of their dreams, extracting them from the lunar womb of their sheets and sending them off to joyless routine, to melancholy jobs and the plastic meatballs of work cafeterias. Now, the barking of the dogs sounds like the growls of factory overseers or the shouts of the police, who, during the university strikes of 1962, their faces protected by a kind of visor, pursued us with batons and tear gas. Soon the sun will cast its cruel light on our shipwreck victims' raft-cum-bed, where we share one last cigarette and one last whisky as if we belonged to a fraternity of beggars, our clothes scattered across the carpet, two bored, naked beggars underneath a bridge, scratching our dusty toes with our grimy fingernails. So, please, if you wouldn't mind, come over here to my side of the bed, sniff the mattress where I have my lair, run your fingers through my hair as if gripped by the gentle, greedy violence of a genuine tenderness, drive out into the corridor the hateful, cruel, pestilential stench of war, and invent a diaphanous childhood peace for our devastated bodies.

V

Does the name Malanje mean anything to you? I was waiting for morning before telling you about Malanje, waiting for the polar, crepuscular unreality that enfolds objects and faces in the same kind of transparent halo that perches on the tops of pine trees in Beira, waiting for the morning, for the listening, breathing, calm sea silence of morning, in order to talk to you about Malanje. Malanje, you see, is now the heap of rubble and ruins that the civil war made of it, a place made unrecognizable by the stupid, pointless violence of the bombs, a flat land filled with corpses, the smoking ribs of houses, and death. Perhaps even then, when I passed through it on my way back to my own country, I could sense the rubble and the ruins beneath the still-intact shapes of the buildings, the trees in the park, the cafés full of pretentious mulattos, whose huge, expensive cars rested the shark snouts of their headlights on the pavement. Perhaps beneath the apparent health of the sun, I could foresee its imminent death, just as certain patients reveal to us, behind their cheery smile and their eyes filled with false hope, the grimace, not of fear or disgust, but of shame, pain and death. The shame of being confined to bed, of being weak, of having to disappear soon, the shame of death, of being seen by others, those who watch from the foot of the bed with the relieved horror of survivors, who invent words of painful optimism and speak in low voices with the nurse in one corner of the room, lit by the diagonal light of an illusory day. Yes, Malanje is now the heap of rubble and ruins that the civil war made of it, a devastated, vanished city, a Temple of Diana with blackened, toppled walls, but in 1973, at the beginning of 1973, it was the land of diamonds, of those who grew rich and fat on diamond smuggling, on *camanga*, the furtive trade in gemstones: everyone carried bottles of reagent in their pockets, the blacks, the whites, the police, the PIDE agents, the administrators, the teachers, the soldiers, and, at night, on the grubby outskirts of villages, protected by the attentive knives of their accomplices, they would buy gems from anyone crossing the river or the frontier with something glassy and glittering wrapped in bits of cloth. Villages and whorehouses under the eucalyptuses, cotton bedcovers, dolls, prematurely old women with silver teeth, record players blasting out the cardiac dance music of the Congo, and the happiness, costing just two hundred *escudos*, of hearing the sudden giggle of a young black woman, her gleeful, mocking laugh as she let you enter her.

Malanje was the small, bald, wrinkled officer standing at the door of the school to watch the girls coming out of class, licking his cigarette paper with an old man's leering lust, or installed after supper on the pavement opposite the mess verandah, ogling, with the protuberant eyes of a stuffed animal, his prepubescent neighbor as she cleared the plates from the table. I once saw him in Chiúme open his fly in front of a female prisoner, force her to place one foot on the rim of the bidet, and then, his beret still on his head, penetrate her, all the while snorting like some repellent, asthmatic goat.

I happened to walk into the sergeants' bathroom, into the eternally flooded, stinking pigsty known as the sergeants' bathroom, and saw the officer clutching the prisoner to him in a kind of epileptic frenzy, the shy, silent girl was leaning against the tiled wall, her eyes blank, and above their heads, through the window, the plain opened out in a majestic fan of subtle shades of green, where one could make out the slow, zigzagging, almost metallic sheen of the river and the great peace of Angola at five in the afternoon, refracted through successive, contradictory layers of mist. The man's buttocks were moving like a piston in a hurry, there were blurred islands of sweat on his shirt where it stuck to his back, his jaw trembled like those of the aged eating lunch in an old-folks' home, the prisoner's blank eyes were staring at me with unbearable fixity, and do you know what, I felt like getting my cock out too and urinating on them for as long as I could, like when I was a child and I used to pee on the toads in the garden, where they sat like frightened, breathing stones, wedged between two tree trunks.

But we couldn't urinate on the war, on the vileness and corruption of the war: it was the war that was urinating on us with its shrapnel and its bullets, imprisoning us in that narrow state of anguish and turning us into sad, resentful creatures, raping women against the white, gleaming cold of tiled walls, or masturbating in bed at night while we waited for the next attack, heavy with resignation and whisky, huddled in the sheets like terrified fetuses, listening to the airy fingers of the wind in the eucalyptuses, just like fingers lightly brushing the keys of a piano made of silent leaves. We have no trees here, only the dust from the buildings they're erecting around this one, in the same depressingly similar style, fit for melancholic bank clerks, and the lights of Areeiro, as blue and cloudy as the eyes of blind dogs, and Avenida Almirante Reis with its shops closed in on themselves like the fists of a sleeping child: people wake up, open the curtains, peer out, see the gray roads, the gray cars, the gray silhouettes walking grayly along, feel stirring inside them an equally gray despair and then, resigned, go back to bed, muttering gray words in their thickening sleep.

Did you realize that I live in a Pompeii of buildings under construction, of walls, beams, growing piles of rubble, abandoned cranes, piles of sand, and cement mixers like round, rusty stomachs? In a few hours' time, workmen wearing hard hats will start hammering away at these ruins perched on future window frames, pneumatic drills will bite into the concrete with stubborn rage, the plumbers will open up networks of arteries in the stiff flesh of the houses. I live in a dead world, with no smells, a world of dust and stone, where the male nurse from the polyclinic who lives on the first floor walks around in his dressing gown, wearing the surprised expression of a bearded faun, looking in vain for some soft, grassy bank to lie on. I live in a world of dust, stone, and trash, mainly trash, trash from the construction sites, trash from the clandestine slums being built, trash from the somersaulting bits of paper that chase each other along the fences and the gutters, blown about by a nonexistent breath, trash from the black-garbed gypsies who live in hollows in the ground, waiting with the immemorial patience of wise apostles.

I wanted to talk to you about Malanje, now that I've acquitted myself reasonably well, you even groaned a couple of times, the yelps of a contented puppy, you writhed as if you had a touch of St. Vitus' dance or were having a fainting fit, your face, eyes closed, mouth open, resembled for a moment the old ladies I used to watch taking Communion when I was a child, old ladies with loose dentures and with their tongues stuck out, eager for the white circle of the host. As a choirboy, I used to help the priest and would observe, fascinated, the extraordinary length of their tongues, those old ladies pushing and elbowing each other, armed with bone-handled umbrellas and large rosaries like the necklaces worn by actresses, while the priest, chalice in hand, muttered mystical belches, barely opening his mouth. I wanted to talk to you about Malanje, about that town surrounded by whorehouses and eucalyptuses, the homeland of the diamond-smuggling trade and garrulous or guarded adventurers, guys with cautious, oblique eyes, sitting casually on café terraces. I wanted to talk to you about the miraculous light in Malanje that seemed to burst out of the earth with impetuous, violent joy, out of that PIDE bunker and the pretentious barracks beneath, a provincial barracks, you see, that stank of indifference and sergeants.

The two hundred fifty miles of road from Malanje to Luanda crossed the amazing Salazar hills, past villages that sat by the roadside like warts around a mouth, past the majestic flow of the River Dondo, where one can sense the presence of the sea in the slow languid movements of its flanks and in the long-legged white birds from the bay of Luanda, brushing the surface of the water with their spindle-shaped Styrofoam bodies. But what mattered in Malanje were the minutes just before dawn, the unreal, poignant, absurd minutes that precede the dawn, as colorless and distorted as the faces of insomnia or fear, the deserted streets, the numb silence of the trees and their branches that seemed to shrink hesitantly back, bruised by an irrational panic. Before dawn, as you know, all towns grow uneasy, they wrinkle in discomfort like the eyelids of a man who has not slept, they watch the light, the indecisive birth of the light, they shudder like sickly pigeons on a rooftop fluttering their night wings, afraid for their own fragile, hollow bones. Pale and orange-colored, as if sketched in pencil on a sky of faded silver, the early sun slowly emerges from the geometric confusion of houses, shriveled squares, shrunken avenues, and cramped streets and finds shadows bereft of mystery taking shelter in living rooms among the glint of wineglasses and the framed smiles of the dead, among mustaches arched like the sarcastic eyebrows of a math teacher who has just presented his students with a particularly difficult problem that involves calculating how long two different faucets will take to fill a bathtub. All towns grow uneasy, but Malanje, you see, trembled as it bent over itself just as I, in bed, bend over you, dreading the day that awaits me, feeling its unbearable stone weight on my chest and the ash that accumulates on my hands, which I wash off in restaurant restrooms before sitting down to the eternally tasteless beef of lunchtime. I would like to ask you not to leave, but to keep me company, to stay lying here with me, waiting not just for the morning but for the next night and the next and the next, because isolation and loneliness are forming a knot in my guts, in my belly, in my arms, in my throat, they're preventing me from moving and speaking, turning me into a tormented vegetable incapable of a shout or a gesture, waiting for the sleep that refuses to come. Stay here with me until I do finally fall asleep and turn away from you with the inexplicable undulating movement of a drowned man washed up in the shallows, and lie facedown on the pillow, burbling indistinguishably, and plunge into the swampy well of a kind of death, snoring in the heavy coma induced by pills and alcohol. Stay with me now that the morning of Malanje is growing and vibrating inside me, in inverted, distorted mirror images, and I'm alone on the city's tarmac streets, near the cafés and the park, filled by a strange, objectless desire, ill-defined but intense, thinking about Lisbon, about Gija or the sea, thinking about the whorehouses under the eucalyptus trees and their beds full of dolls and doilies. The fear of returning to my country makes my throat tighten because, you see, I have no place anywhere, I went too far away for too long ever to belong here again, to these autumns of rain and Sunday Masses, these long winters as dull as blown light-bulbs, these faces that I can barely recognize beneath all the lines and wrinkles, clearly invented by some ironic caricaturist. Root-less, I float between two continents, both of which spurn me, I'm searching for an empty space in which I might drop anchor and which could, for example, be the long mountain range of your body, some recess or hollow in your body where I could lay my shamefaced hope.

X

---

*N*o, really, listen: now that we're about to part, having arranged a vague rendezvous in some vague restaurant of which we'll have no recollection tomorrow, now that we won't see each other again, apart from some fleeting, chance encounter in a bar or a cinema, with just enough time to wave and smile, one of those instantaneous, affectless smiles that opens and closes like a camera shutter over a circular gleam of teeth, now that you're about to put your clothes back on with the hasty, neutral gestures of a woman getting off a gynecologist's examining table, doing up your buttons as if you were stapling yourself together, while I lean on one elbow on the mattress, next to the ashtray overflowing with ashes and cigarette ends, from which there arises the awful cold-tobacco smell of things that are over, now I can confess that I like you. Seriously. I like the attentive irony of your silence, the laughter that occasionally hovers over your features when in repose, like an undecided cloud, I like your exotic bracelets, the appraising glint in your eyes, your limber thighs that close around my body the way water, in one single, soundless movement, covers the last limp seaweed wave with which the drowned dissolve into weightless foam. I like the night spent by your side, as slow and heavy as the sleeping nape of a neck, I like imagining you coming straight back here with a suitcase full of clothes, standing on the doormat and fixing me with a gaze that is at once piercing and dark with passion, and the two of us staying here together, locked in an embrace, in this sad, furnitureless apartment, looking out at the river, where the colored lights coagulate, pulsating and blinking, like veins under the pressure of a shadowy finger. Together we would create exquisite meals in the kitchen, mingling bottles, seasonings, and kisses over the pots on the stove, we would flood the rooms with lazy Asian odors, frivolous magazines, and children's drawings, we would count each other's gray hairs with the innocent joy of old age averted, you would squeeze my blackheads, I would run my tongue between your excited toes, and we would fall asleep on the carpet, ignoring the bed, the demands of work, the robotic tyranny of the alarm clock, and we would feel, if not happy exactly, at least, how can I put it, pleasantly satiated.

Forgive me for going on at you like this, but I'm so tired of being alone, so tired of the tragic, ridiculous farce of my life, of the shredded-beef sandwich I have for lunch every day in the snack bar, and of the cleaning lady who works and cleans far less than I pay her to, so tired that sometimes, you know, just as certain animals grow weary of the garbage they live amongst, I feel like ditching all the nauseating distress and disorder on which I feed and to be able, instead, to stand in front of the mirror, whistling, filled by an immaculate contentment. I feel like vomiting into the toilet bowl the discomfort of the daily death I carry with me like an acid stone in my stomach, which spreads through my veins and slides into my limbs with a terrifying, oily fluidity, I feel like returning, well groomed and healthy, to the starting line where a circle of pleasant, compassionate faces awaits me, my family, my brothers, my friends, my daughters, the strangers who expect from me what, out of shyness or vanity, I could never give them, and offer them the lucidity untainted by resentment and the warmth free of cynicism of which I have never before felt capable. I feel like driving out those stiff corpses sitting on my chairs in pale, tenacious expectation, my mother walking straight past me, her mind on something else, my father glancing up from his armchair and looking through me without even seeing me, my brothers caught up in their strange inner tangles that could never be undone, the upright pianos covered in damask throws whose Chopins bind me with narcissistic melancholy, I want Isabel, the reality of Isabel, the reality independent of me of Isabel, Isabel's teeth, Isabel's laugh, Isabel's breasts like the noses of gazelles beneath the man's shirt she sometimes wore, her hands on my buttocks when we made love, and her eyelids that trembled and shook like a sheet of fine stationery pierced by a cruel pin.

You can turn out the light if you like: I don't need it now. When I think about Isabel, I stop feeling afraid of the dark, an amber-yellow light clothes everything in the companionable serenity of July mornings, whose childlike sun I always felt placed before me the necessary materials to build something so ineffably lovely that even I would never be able to explain it away. The Isabel who replaced my paralyzed dreams with her gently implacable pragmatism could stitch up the cracks in my existence with the quick thread of two or three decisions whose simplicity astonished me, and then, suddenly a girl again, she would lie down on top of me, take my face in her hands, and say, Let me kiss you, in a tiny beseeching voice that made my heart turn over. I think I lost her in the same way I lose everything, drove her away with my mood swings, my unexpected rages, my absurd demands, the anxious thirst for tenderness that repels affection and lingers, throbbing painfully, in the form of a mute appeal full of a prickly, irrational hostility. And I remember, with emotion, with pain, the house in the Algarve surrounded by crickets and fig trees, the warm night sky tinged by the distant glow of the sea, the whitewashed walls almost phosphorescent in the dark, and the violent, unformulated passion of my caresses that seemed to stop, irresolute, inches from her face and dissolve at last into some undefined gesture. I think of Isabel, and a kind of tide, tense with love, untamed and vigorous, rises up my legs to my penis, makes my testicles grow hard with desire, spreads to my belly as if it were opening great calm wings in my warring guts. We again go searching Sintra's dusty antiques shops for carved wooden furniture, we enter the blue aquarium of the nightclub where, astonished, I touched her mouth for the first time, we invent a fantastic future of dark-haired children in a profusion of cribs, and I feel happy, justified and happy, when I embrace her body in the shallows of the sheets, of which the creases are the waves washing up on the white beach of the pillow, where our heads, hers dark and mine fair, meet in a fusion that contains within it the strange germ of a miracle.

You can turn out the light now: perhaps I won't feel so alone now in this enormous room, perhaps Isabel or you will come back one day to visit me, perhaps I'll hear a voice over the phone, a voice made minutely precise by the plastic holes in the receiver, her Hello or your Hello entering my ear with the pleasant oily feel of the drops they used to put in my ears when I was a child to soften the wax, perhaps I'll pick you or her up at work, waiting in the car, impatiently smoking, straining upward with a tightening of the buttocks so that I can see in the rearview mirror to straighten my tie, perhaps she or you will get into the car in the dark, will smile at me, lean over to slot a tape of Maria Bethânia* into the cassette player, and encircle my neck with the firm elbows of tenderness. Let me kiss you. Let me kiss you while you're getting dressed, while you fasten your bra behind you with blind, awkward gestures that make your shoulder blades stick out like chicken wings, while you're feeling for your silver rings on the bedside table, one small childish frown line between your brows, while you're struggling with the brush against the wavy resistance of your hair, the thick hair that my bald head envies with a ferocity I can't quite shake off. Every morning I wonder to myself when I will begin parting my hair just above my ear, laboriously dragging one thin lock over my bare pate, and start to read, without irony now, the advertisements for toupees in the newspaper, which are always accompanied by photographs of smug, hairy bald men with hairy gorilla smiles. I am leaving behind me last year's photographs like a boat leaving the dock, and sometimes I feel that I'm becoming a strange caricature of myself, which the lines on my face distort into a pastiche of various grimaces. Let me kiss you: what woman would want to kiss this sad parody of the man I once was, the protruding belly, the thinning legs, the empty bag of testicles overgrown with a leather-colored mane? On second thought, don't turn out the light: perhaps this morning conceals inside it a darker night than all the nights I have so far known, the one that lives in the bottom of whisky bottles, unmade beds, and other objects that speak of absence, a night with an ice cube floating on the surface above three fingers of yellow liquid that contains an unbearable silence in its empty interior,

---

* Maria Bethânia (b. 1946) is one of Brazil's most popular singers and the sister of famed musician Caetano Veloso.

a night in which I get lost, bumping against the walls, befuddled with alcohol, giving myself the usual speech about how terribly lonely I am that is common to all drunks, for whom the world is the reflected image of giants against which, pointlessly, they rail.

No, don't turn out the light: when you leave, the apartment will inevitably grow in size, becoming a kind of waterless swimming pool in which the sounds boom and echo, aggressive, hard, enormous, hurling themselves violently against my body like the equinoctial tides against the seawall, drenching me in the dingy foam of syllables. I will once again listen to the fermenting sounds coming from the icebox, like the purr of a sleeping mammoth, the drops that escape from the edges of faucets like the tears of the very old, heavy with a rusty conjunctivitis. I will hesitate in my shirt, tie, and suit and then end up slamming the street door as if I were leaving behind me an intact tomb in which death blooms in the cut-glass vases, among the rotten stems of the chrysanthemums. Yes, slamming the street door, just as I slammed the door of Africa when I returned to Lisbon, the ghastly door of war, the whores in Luanda, and the coffee-plantation owners sitting beside their champagne ice buckets, as glittering as the sequined boxes of illusionists, smoking contraband American cigarettes in the gloom of a tango. The door of Africa, Isabel: a homosexual doctor—whose eyelashes are so long they form knots like octopus tentacles—assisted by a facetious, sideburn-wearing corporal with whom he doubtless gets together in boardinghouses with a little exhausted sigh like the sound of a rubber sucker, is examining our piss, our shit, our blood, so that we won't go and infect Our Country with our fear of death, the memory of the fair-haired kid lying dead under a blanket in my room, the eucalyptuses in Ninda and the nurse sitting on the path with his intestines in his hands, staring at us with the sad horror of an animal. Our blood is clean, Isabel: the blood tests don't show the blacks digging their own graves before being shot by the PIDE, nor the man hanged by the inspector in Chiquita, nor Ferreira's leg in the dressing bucket, nor the bones of that guy in Mangando embedded in the corrugated iron roof. Our blood is as clean as that of the generals in their air-conditioned offices in Luanda, sticking colored pins in the map of Angola, as clean as that of the gentlemen who got rich selling helicopters and arms in Lisbon, the war is fought in the assholes of the world, you see, not in this colonial city that I loathe, the war is those colored pins on the map of Angola and the humiliated Angolans, numb with hunger behind the wire fence, it's having ice cubes shoved up your ass, it's the extraordinary endless depths of those fixed, unmoving calendars.

Sometimes, you know, I wake in the middle of the night and sit up, eyes wide open, and I seem to hear, coming from the bathroom, or from the corridor, or from the living room, or from the girls' bunk beds, the soft call of the dead in those lead coffins, with the metal dog tag we all had to wear placed on their tongues like a metal Communion wafer. I seem to hear the whispering leaves of the mango trees in Marimba and see their vast silhouettes against the misty sky, I seem to hear the sudden, proudly free laughter of the Luchazi, which bursts forth next to me like Dizzy Gillespie's trumpet, gushing out of the silence like a burst artery. I wake in the middle of the night, and knowing that my piss and my shit and my blood are clean doesn't calm me or make me happy: I'm sitting with the lieutenant outside the abandoned mission, time has stopped on every clock, on your wristwatch, on the alarm clock, on the radio, on the watch that Isabel probably uses now and that I've never seen, on the broken but still ticking clock that exists in the minds of the dead, the pollen from the acacias wraps us lightly in weightless, noiseless gold, the afternoon slips through the grass with an animal languor, I get up to piss against the wall and my pee is clean, irreprehensibly clean, I can return to Lisbon without alarming anyone, without contaminating anyone with my dead, with the memory of my dead comrades, I can go back to Lisbon and enter restaurants, bars, cinemas, hotels, supermarkets, and hospitals, and everyone can be quite sure that my shit and my ass are clean, because no one can open up my skull and see the medic scraping at his boots with a stick and saying over and over Fuck fuck fuck fuck fuck, as he sits crouched on the steps of the administrator's office.

Even so, I took care to say good-bye to the bay, that shell of putrid water full of the shimmering, upside-down reflections of buildings. The trawlers were leaving the harbor to go fishing, the dull, irregular sound of their engines startling the great white birds as they strutted about in the mud with the proprietorial strides of managers, and ruffling the tousled, drooping hair of the palm trees that cast narrow shadows onto the deserted benches. In the café in the arcade, black street vendors were trying to palm people off with the illusory Band-Aids of their ghastly fetishes. Bootblacks slouched among the tables, bent over glittering shoes. The homosexual doctor, sitting on the chair next to mine, languidly lit a gold filter cigarette and blew out the match with a delicate pout of his lips. He wore the heavy perfume of a maiden cousin, filling the air, like incense, with large, gaseous, sugary exhalations. We had met in London, in the grizzled autumn of St. James's Park, we had shared the same rented room, and I had watched his complicated daily ritual, involving creams, brushes, tweezers, and the tortoiseshell boxes of beauty products, which he handled with the dexterous patience of a Vermeer, creating a made-up face that looked as if it had slipped furtively out of a vampire movie. His underwear resembled the outfits worn by trapeze artistes at the circus, lit by the admiring, ecstatic lilac of the spotlight. In a way, we liked each other because our respective solitudes, his smug and mine angry, touched and converged at one common point, possibly our resigned lack of resignation. He was so feminine that, in uniform, he looked like a female police officer. He raised his cigarette to his lips as cautiously as if it were a very hot cup of tea, then slid me a glance of his large, tender, knowingly innocent eyes:

"How are you going to survive in Lisbon after being out here in this asshole of the world?"

The streetlights along the coast road suddenly came on, as one, and thousands of insects immediately thronged the bluish cones of light, as frenetic as the flashing neon bulbs on the marquees of cinemas. The distant clatter of cutlery announced that it was supper time.

"Oh, I'll just take it slowly," I said, brushing away with my hand the shattered bodies on the jungle path. "You yourself said that I have clean blood."

1

---

*W*ait, I'll see you to the door. I'm sorry it's taking me so long to get out of bed, and I do hope that, rather than seeing this as bad manners, you'll view it merely as the regrettable result of an excess of whisky, a sleepless night, and the emotional exhaustion of telling you this long story that is now reaching its end. Besides, it's light now: out in the street, you can clearly hear the trucks arriving at the construction site and the flushing of a toilet somewhere upstairs announcing that the neighbors are stirring. Everything is real now: the furniture, the walls, our tiredness, this city crowded with monuments and people, like a sideboard topped with too many knick-knacks, which I lovingly detest. Everything is real: I touch my face and the rasp of my unshaven cheek scratches my hand, my full bladder swells my belly with its warm liquid, heavy as a round, grumbling fetus. An oblique ray of light anemically illuminates a patch of wallpaper next to the closet and very slowly travels down to the carpet, to the gray reflector of the electric heater and the elegantly bowed legs of the rocking chair, where my clothes hang in the forgotten disorder of rags. Equally real are the yellow stains on the stucco ceiling, which I can see clearly now, the smiles of my daughters in their framed photographs, and the telephone that, you might say, is always on the verge of flying into a rage, ready to burst into shrill, furious ringing. Your impatience is real too, as is the handbag over your shoulder, your well-turned ankles, which I hadn't noticed until now, trembling with haste in their shoes. It's not going to rain today: I can feel it in my calm, tranquil bones, slightly weary from so many hours without rest, yes, I can feel it in my light, dry, hard bones, as porous as pumice, which are asking me, from inside my body, to float from carpet to carpet with the stumbling grace of an angel, my toenails brushing the shadows in the tunnel of the corridor. It's not going to rain: the pink sky, as empty as the roof of a toothless mouth, is growing thick with heat along the broken line where it's touched by the rooftops, taking on a red-green tone that inflames the terraces, the balconies, and the exaggeratedly clear edge of the buildings in the distance. By two in the afternoon, the trees will be sweating resin from their scorched trunks, the bronze of the statues in the squares will bend like molten iron, with the flaccid obedience of weary gestures. You'll go home, take a quick shower, choose a dress from the showcase of sleeves hanging side by side in the closet, and before leaving for work, you'll disguise the shadows under your eyes with the enormous dark glasses, which, if you don't mind my saying, make you resemble some haughty insect. I'm fascinated and intrigued by what goes on behind the dark glasses of the women I pass in the streets of Lisbon: their opaque, expressionless faces provoke in me a desire to remove, very delicately, those bits of brown or green glass, in order to see what lies behind, be it panic, tenderness, indifference, or sarcasm, anything, in short, that will guarantee they share the same humanity as me, rather than the Martian condition I imagine to be theirs. And apartments, at around supper time, lit by the sweetly domestic light of lampshades and by the rectangular phosphorescence of television screens, make me feel hopelessly excluded from thousands of small, comfortable universes of which I would love to be a part, sitting on a sofa, opposite a Miró reproduction, my cowed, shamefaced loneliness making me constantly bend my submissive back, pretending annoyance. Furniture stores that display posters of stereotypically domestic scenes, showing a girl and a kitten tenderly embracing, for example, have always delighted me: don't tell anyone, but the happiness revealed in one of those full-color folding leaflets constitutes my main goal in life, and my long-term plan is to replace the complicated writing desks of the soul with plastic shelves, black-and-white-check cushions, oval rugs with a pile as thick as my uncles' eyebrows, and large, amorphous ceramic objects decorated with random daubs of paint. No, listen, such a scenario really might insinuate itself into our existence, filling it with sardonic clay masks and strange angular lamps bristling with springs, and a paint-thick blood might start to flow through our veins, lining them with a metallic joy, proof against the damp of tears. I'm going to buy a porcelain Bambi for the desk in my office, I'll place it right in front of my papers and my books, between me and the river, and then you'll see the radical change in direction my life will take, carrying me off to a future as a bullfighter or a radio singer, sitting by my private pool with my arm around a smiling blonde.

Yes, everything is real: the tinkling of your bracelets sounds different, stripped of the mysterious reverberations and echoes conferred on it by the night, now it has the banal sound of the morning, which makes suffering and excitement seem merely commonplace and diminishes their importance vis-à-vis the practical demands of everyday life: work, getting the car serviced, going to the dentist, having supper with a garrulous childhood friend, who drones on and on over the knives and forks with his endless, boring stories. Everything is real, especially pain, hangovers, the headache that has the back of my neck in its steely grip, the gestures slowed to a slur by an aquarium torpor that turns my fingers into glass and makes them as difficult to manipulate as the pincers of a prosthetic hand. Everything is real apart from the war, which never existed: there were never any colonies, no Fascism, no Salazar, no Tarrafal prison camp,* no PIDE, no Revolution, nothing, you understand, the calendars of this country stopped moving so long ago that we've forgotten all about them, meaningless Marches and Aprils rot on the tear-off pages of the wall calendar, with the Sundays in red on the left in a useless column. Luanda is an invented city of which I take my leave, and in Mutamba, invented people take invented cars to invented places, where the MPLA is subtly introducing invented political commissars. The plane that brings us back to Lisbon is carrying a cargo of ghosts who slowly materialize, officers and soldiers, yellow with malaria, who sit riveted to their seats, empty eyes staring out the window at the colorless, uterine space of the sky. The gray buses waiting at the airport and the cold of Lisbon are real, as are the sergeants checking our documents with the indolent slowness of bored functionaries, the journey to the barracks where our bags are piled in one confused conical heap, and the rapid farewells on the parade ground.

We spent twenty-seven months together in the asshole of the world, twenty-seven months of anguish and death in the sands of

---

* Tarrafal (also known as "the Camp of Slow Death") was a prison camp in Cape Verde, then a Portuguese colony, set up by the Portuguese dictator Salazar to house opponents of his regime.

Eastern Angola, on the paths left by the Quioco people, and among the sunflowers of Cassanje, we ate the same homesickness, the same shit, the same fear, and yet it took us just five minutes to say good-bye, a handshake, a pat on the back, a vague embrace, and then, bent under the weight of our luggage, we were gone, out through the main gate and off into the civilian whirlwind of the city.

As I stood there, still in uniform, with a bag full of books on one shoulder and another full of clothes in my hand, Lisbon presented me with the opaque face of an insurmountable backdrop, smooth, hostile, vertical, with no windows opening onto cozy future nests on which I could soothe my eyes thirsty for repose. The traffic majestically circles the Rotunda da Encarnação with a purely mechanical indifference that excludes me, the faces in the streets slip past me, utterly oblivious, and there is something in their attitude that reminds me of the geometric inertia of corpses. My green-eyed daughter doubtless considers me an undesirable stranger whose narrow, superfluous body has taken its place beside her mother in bed. My friends' lives, which have grown used to going on without me in my absence, will find it hard to accommodate this newly resuscitated, disoriented Lazarus, who finds it painfully difficult to relearn sounds and the use of certain objects. I had grown too accustomed to the silence and solitude of Angola, and it seemed to me unimaginable that the grass and the scrub would not push up through the tarmac on the avenues with their long, green fingers honed by the first rains. There was no broken-down, rusty sewing machine at my parents' house, and the Chiúme chief wasn't waiting for me in the living room, staring, beyond the bookshelf with the glass doors, at the vastness of the plain, damp with toads and mud. Just as a child gazes, eyes round with surprise, at traffic lights, cinemas, the uneven shapes of city squares, the melancholy terraces of cafés, so it was with me, as if everything around were charged with a mystery I would never be able to comprehend. And so I drew in my head and hunched my shoulders, the way people do when caught in an unexpected shower without a raincoat, and thus, exposing as little as possible of my body to a country I no longer understood, I rushed headlong into the January of the city.

I visited my aunts a few weeks later, wearing a suit from before the war that hung about my waist like a slipped halo, despite the best efforts of my suspenders, which hoisted the legs of my trousers waistward as if they were equipped with an invisible propeller. I waited, standing next to the piano topped by candlesticks, squeezing my timid bones between a bandy-legged antique console table crammed with framed photos of dead generals and an enormous clock whose great heart was gently sobbing out the rhythmic rumbles of a peaceful Buddha digesting his meal. The curtains at the window moved with the evasive, undulating gestures of a bored choreographer, the sharp eyes of the silver on the sideboards glittered in the dark. My aunts turned on the lamp to be able to see me better, and the light revealed faded Arraiolos rugs, the white surfaces of Chinese vases adorned with energetic, fork-tongued dragons, and the curiosity of the maids peering around the door, drying their plump hands on their aprons. Instinctively, I adopted the stiff, serious pose we offer to official photographers as they examine us from behind the thick, pitiless lenses of their tripod cameras, or the pose we adopt when we stand at attention, as I did as a cadet in Mafra, in order to be inspected by the captain's chronic, authoritarian ill humor as he frowned, boots akimbo, in an arrogant attitude that boded no good. The room smelled of camphor, naphthalene, and Siamese cat pee, and I longed furiously to leave there and go out into Rua Alexandre Herculano, where one could at least see, aloft, a murky scrap of sky. In the heavy air of the living room, a cane walking stick performed a scornful arabesque, approached my chest, and buried itself there like a fencing foil, and a frail voice, muffled by false teeth, as if it had come from very far away and very high up, scraped a few wooden syllables against the aluminum spatula of the tongue and said:

"You're thinner. I always hoped that the army would make a man of you, but there's clearly no hope of that."

And the photos of the dead generals on the console tables nodded their fierce agreement with this self-evident misfortune.

No, you go straight on, take the first turn on the right, then the second turn on the right immediately after that, and before you know it, you're in Praceta do Areeiro. Safe and sound. Me? I'm going to hang around here for a while longer. I'll empty the ashtrays, wash the glasses, tidy up the living room, look at the river. I might even go back to my unmade bed, pull the sheets over me, and close my eyes. Besides, who knows, Tia Teresa might drop by and visit me.

About the Translator

Margaret Jull Costa has worked as a translator of Portuguese, Spanish, and Latin-American writers for over twenty years. In 1992 she was joint recipient of the Portuguese Translation Prize for Fernando Pessoa's *The Book of Disquiet*, and in 1997 she won the translator's portion of the International IMPAC Dublin Literary Award for *A Heart So White* by Javier Marías. In 2000 she was awarded the Oxford-Weidenfeld Translation Prize for Nobel Laureate José Saramago's *All the Names*, and in 2006 her translation of Javier Marías's *Your Face Tomorrow: Fever and Spear* won the Premio Valle-Inclán. In 2008, her version of Eça de Queirós's masterpiece, *The Maias*, brought her both the PEN/Book-of-the-Month Club Translation Prize and, for the second time, the Oxford-Weidenfeld Translation Prize. More recently, she won the 2009 and 2010 Premio Valle-Inclán for, respectively, Bernardo Atxaga's *The Accordionist's Son* and Javier Marías's *Your Face Tomorrow: Poison, Shadow, and Farewell*. Other authors whose work she has translated include Ramón del Valle-Inclán, Mário de Sá-Carneiro, Luis Fernando Verissimo, and Lídia Jorge.

The translator would like to thank António Lobo Antunes, Tânia Ganho, and Ben Sherriff for all their help and advice.

About the Author

Born in Lisbon on September 1, 1942, António Lobo Antunes grew up during the repressive years of the Salazar dictatorship. He was 31 when the Carnation Revolution transformed Portugal from a virtual police state into a liberal democracy, but the political repression he experienced during his youth greatly influenced his adult consciousness and would inform much of his fiction.

At the urging of his father, Lobo Antunes opted as a young man to go to medical school, where he specialized in psychiatry. Required to serve in the Army, he became a military doctor in Portugal's doomed colonial war in Angola, an experience that influenced many of his novels. After his return to Lisbon in 1973, he began working as a clinical psychiatrist before devoting himself primarily to literature.

António Lobo Antunes has written 18 novels that have been translated into more than 20 languages. His first novel, *Elephant Memory*, was published in 1979. In the same year, his second novel, *Os Cus de Judas* (first translated into English as *South of Nowhere* and here as *The Land at the End of the World*), was published to international acclaim. His more recent novels, *The Inquisitors' Manual*, about life during the Salazar dictatorship, and *The Return of the Caravels*, about the breakup of Portugal's colonial dominion in the 1970s, have both been named *New York Times* Notable Books of the Year.

António Lobo Antunes is considered by many the greatest novelist on the Iberian Peninsula. For George Steiner he is the "heir to Conrad or Faulkner." In fact, the *Los Angeles Times Book Review* commented that Lobo Antunes writes "with the insight of Faulkner, of a man who knows the scent and taste of the dust from which his characters are begotten."

António Lobo Antunes has received many literary awards, including the Jerusalem Prize for the Freedom of the Individual in Society (2005) and the Camões Prize, the most important literary prize for authors writing in Portuguese (2007). He lives in Lisbon.